murder

in the rue dauphine

murder

in the rue dauphine

by greg herren

 alyson books
los angeles | new york

MANUFACTURED IN THE UNITED STATES OF AMERICA.

THIS TRADE PAPERBACK ORIGINAL IS PUBLISHED BY ALYSON PUBLICATIONS,
P.O. BOX 4371, LOS ANGELES, CA 90078-4371.
DISTRIBUTION IN THE UNITED KINGDOM BY
TURNAROUND PUBLISHER SERVICES LTD.,
UNIT 3, OLYMPIA TRADING ESTATE, COBURG ROAD, WOOD GREEN,
LONDON N22 6TZ ENGLAND.

FIRST EDITION: JANUARY 2002

02 03 04 05 06 a 10 9 8 7 6 5 4 3 2 1

ISBN 1-55583-585-6

LIBRARY OF CONGRESS CATALOGING-IN-PUBLICATION DATA
HERREN, GREG.
    MURDER IN THE RUE DAUPHINE / GREG HERREN. — 1ST ED.
    ISBN 1-55583-585-6
      1. PRIVATE INVESTIGATORS — LOUISIANA — NEW ORLEANS — FICTION.
  2. NEW ORLEANS (LA.) — FICTION. 3. HATE CRIMES — FICTION. 4. GAY MEN —
  FICTION. I. TITLE.
  PS3608.E64 M87 2002
  813'.6 — DC21   2001045824

COVER DESIGN BY LOUIS MANDRAPILIAS.
COVER PHOTOGRAPHY BY JOHNATHAN BLACK.

This is for Paul with all my love

No writer is an island, and throughout my turbulent, occasionally troubled life, any number of people have kept me and my dream of being a published author alive through their love, encouragement, belief, and support. So, I would like to thank Josh Solomon, Bill and Kara Warnke, Rees and Diane Warne, Craig Freeman, Dawn Lobaugh, Karen Bengtsen, Sally Anderson, Janna Davidson Sill, Ed Watson, Cheryl Filipiak, Barbara Bryan, Richard and Laurie Stepanski, Tamra Lukes, Michael Kooiman, Robin and Lou Ann Morehouse, Melinda Shelton, Richard Schneider, Felice Picano, William J. Mann, Dorothy Allison, Kevin Allman, J.M. Redmann, Melissa Smallwood, Danny Fisher, Lisa Anderson, Carrie Anderson, and anyone I have forgotten, you know who you are.

I would also like to thank my first writing teacher in college (who told me I would never be a writer) for inspiring me to never give up.

If it weren't for Julie Smith this book would never have been written. She is an amazing talent, an incredible friend, an inspiration, and a truly great lady.

My best friend, Marika Christian, always believed in me and always kept pushing me to write, even on the darkest days when I was convinced that it was all a pipe dream that would never amount to anything. Bless you, Marika, every writer should have a friend like you.

Dan Cullinane has been a joy to work with for the last four years and without his advice and support, this book would have never been published.

My editor, Scott Brassart, who is an angel in human guise.

And finally, my partner, Paul Willis, who put up with the dark days, made the good days that much better, and believed in me enough to make any number of personal sacrifices so that I could write this book. Thanks for grounding me and making me happier than I ever believed possible.

CHAPTER ONE

Never come to New Orleans in the summer. It's hot. It's humid. It's sticky. It's damp. It's hot. Air conditioners blow on high. Ceiling fans rotate. Nothing helps. The air is thick as syrup. Sweat becomes a given. No antiperspirant works. Aerosols, sticks, powders, and creams all fail. The thick air just hangs there, brooding. The sun shows no mercy. The vegetation grows out of control. Everything's wet. The buildings perspire. Even a simple task becomes a chore. Taking the garbage out becomes an ordeal. The heat makes the garbage rot faster. The city starts to smell sour. The locals try to mask the smell of sweat with more perfume. Hair spray sales go up. Women turn their hair into lacquered helmets that start to sag after an hour or so.

Even the flies get lazy.

My sinuses were giving me fits as I left the airport and headed into the city. It was only 7 o'clock in the morning but already hotter than hell. The air was thick. I reached for the box of tissue under my seat and blew my nose. The pressure in my ears popped. Blessed relief.

As I drove alongside the runways I could see a Transco Airlines 737 taxiing into takeoff position. I saluted as I drove past, thinking it might be the flight that my current lover was working. Paul looked good in the uniform. It takes a great body to look sexy in polyester. He does.

He'd be gone for four days on this trip. I was at loose ends. I'd wrapped up a security job for Crown Enterprises the previous Wednesday. The big check that I'd banked guaranteed I wouldn't have to worry about money for a while. I like when money's not a concern.

Paul and I had just gotten back from a long weekend on South Beach. My skin was tanned a nice deep brown. It'd been fun—lying on the beach catching the Atlantic breeze, jumping into the warm water of the Gulf Stream and looking at the endless parade of tanned, sculpted male bodies wearing thongs that bared their hard butts. Funny how that gets old after a while. They begin to look alike after an hour or so. Now I was back, Paul was on a plane, and I had time on my hands.

I had the car's air-conditioning on high, and I was still sweating.

There weren't a lot of cars heading into the city yet. It was still too early for the I-10 traffic to tangle and snarl. In another hour the highway would be clogged with commuters heading in for their day jobs from the burbs and from across the lake. I couldn't do it. The whole idea of living in the burbs, driving in daily, then driving back every night has never made sense to me. For me, to live in New Orleans means living in New Orleans. So there's a crime problem? Get over it.

The thing about New Orleans that outsiders never grasp is that it's just a small town. Everyone knows everyone. If you don't know someone, you've heard more about them than you care to. My landlady once told me, "This town is about a block long, and everyone's on a damn party line."

I lasted two years as a cop here. I've never taken well to

authority or to being ruled by a time clock. When I'd had it, I got my P.I. license and quit. I set my business up in my apartment on Coliseum Square in the lower Garden District. I'd saved up enough money to keep myself going if I didn't get any jobs right away, but I got lucky.

My landlady, Barbara Castlemaine, was being black-mailed. I took care of that problem for her. It was easier than I'd thought it would be. Then I designed a security system for Bodytech, my gym. That brought in a nice chunk of change.

Chanse MacLeod, Private Detective, was off and running.

I got off the highway and turned right at Magazine. I fig-ured since I was going to be up this early I might as well get my workout over. I headed down Magazine Street into the Garden District.

I pulled into the parking lot of the gym, shut off my engine, and walked over to PJ's to get a cup of coffee. I love their coffee. My favorite is the dark French roast with chicory, but whatever dark roast they had for the day was fine with me. I opened the door and walked in. It was too early yet for a line, but by 8 A.M. there would be a 15- to 20-minute wait. We take our coffee seriously here. I ordered a large, hot cup of dark Vienna. As I said, I love coffee, and it better be hot. Many natives abandon hot coffee during the hellish summer months. They switch to iced coffee. Wimps. Not me. I like my coffee hot and steaming. I don't care if I sweat buckets while drinking it.

I walked into the gym. The stereo was blasting the Pet Shop Boys. I glanced around to see if anyone I knew was working out. I was relieved that I didn't recognize the guy doing leg extensions. I liked working out in the mornings because the gym was usually empty. I'm not into all the socializing most people go to the gym for. I go to work out, not for idle chatter. A lot of straight people worked out there, but the vast majority of the clientele was gay.

"Morning, Alan," I said, handing him my membership card.

"Nice tan," he said as he checked my card against the computer. Alan Gardner owned the gym. He always does this, even though he knows who I am and that my membership is always up to date. Alan is dirty blond, with green eyes and a pretty nice body that he works out five times a week. He'd be cute if he didn't have such big teeth. When he smiles he looks a little chipmunkish. Maybe it's the dimples. "How was South Beach?"

"Nice," I said. "Everyone on the beach looked like either a stripper or a porn star."

"That's South Beach." Alan gave me the chipmunk grin. "Greg and I might head down there next month for a little rest and relaxation. Paul flying the friendly skies again?"

Paul and I had met at the gym when he first moved into town five weeks earlier. "Yeah. Four days this trip."

"It must suck to let that stud go away all the time." Alan shook his head.

I headed for the locker room to throw my gym bag in a locker. The locker room is pretty basic. Eighty metal lockers, some benches to sit on, and then a tile floor leading back to the showers, sauna, hot tub, and steam room. There was another guy in there, tying a shoelace. "Hey," he said, without looking up. He had great legs.

"Hey," I said absently. I took out my headphones, then shoved my bag into a locker. The music Alan plays is pumping, but I wear my headphones and listen to tapes. I don't want to listen to other people grunting and groaning and dropping weights. It's distracting. I walked back out into the gym and got on a stair climber. I always warm up that way. The tape I had in my Walkman was playing an old Madonna remix. I started climbing, my eyes closed, losing myself in the music and the rhythm of my legs. I was vaguely aware of someone next to me. I lost myself in the music and the movement.

After 10 minutes, I climbed off and walked to a free area to stretch. I felt good. The coffee was starting to kick in. I took a look at the guy still climbing. He looked familiar, but then everyone does in New Orleans. I sat there for a moment. Where had I seen him before? Think, think. I saw him in my mind, dancing at Oz with his shirt off. I concentrated. His first name was Mike. We'd never met, but several people I knew were in lust with him. Small wonder. I had seen him frequently with a guy named Ronnie Bishop, a born asshole, in the bars. I'd heard somewhere that Ronnie was his boyfriend.

He looked up, caught me looking at him, and smiled. It was a cute smile, which spread across his face and made his blue eyes light up. Dimples deepened in his cheeks on both sides below strong cheekbones. Small, even white teeth appeared between his lips. His dark hair was cut short, almost military style. It emphasized the squareness of his jaw. He looked like the perfect soldier in an extremely butch comic book, like Sergeant Rock. He was wearing a ribbed tank top that stretched tightly across the swell of his big chest. It also made his arms look huge. He was wearing a pair of black boxer shorts that clung tightly where the powerful legs came out. A line of sweat was developing on his tank top in the deep cleavage between his pectorals. *Damn, he's got a fine body,* I thought. He was built kind of like Paul, only Paul was taller and not as stocky. Paul was about 5 foot 10, and this guy could be no more than 5 foot 7 max. His skin was a light pinkish white, the kind that doesn't tan but burns easily. There was a scattering of freckles across the bridge of his nose. He finished and walked toward me.

Because of my police training, I have a tendency to catalog people by height and looks.

I took my headphones off.

He said, "You're Chanse MacLeod, right?"

I stood. At 6 foot 3, I towered over him. "Yeah, that's right. And your name is Mike?"

"That's right, Mike Hansen." He grinned at me as we shook hands. His hands were surprisingly big. His grip was strong and firm. His voice was higher pitched than I like in a man but not effeminate.

"I hear you're a pretty good detective."

"I like to think so."

He scratched the top of his head, and his smile faded away. "I, um, I may need to hire a detective."

"What seems to be the trouble, Mike?"

"I'd rather not talk about it here." He glanced around to see who was listening. I looked around as well. Alan was at the counter reading the latest muscle magazine. The guy who'd been doing leg extensions when I first arrived was on the other side of the gym doing calf raises. "You want to maybe work out together? Then I'll buy you breakfast, and we can talk."

I don't usually like to work out with anyone. Then again, he was a potential client. "OK."

An hour and a half later, I was drenched in sweat and exhausted. Mike was not one of those people who go to the gym to socialize and gossip, either. He moved from exercise to exercise with few breaks between sets. We worked on chest, triceps, and back. By the time we were finished, I was afraid my arms would be too tired to steer my car. Mike was also sweaty and exhausted, but he grinned at me as we headed for the locker room. "You've got a great body. If you pushed it, you could be huge."

I looked at him. I'd thought my own routine was pretty grueling. "Do you want to compete in bodybuilding?"

He looked startled. "Oh, no, I just like lifting weights. I like feeling sore, you know? It's pretty crazy, I know, but I've always liked it. I started when I was 13, and I've worked out about five days a week ever since."

That was a first. Of all the reasons to work out, I'd never met someone who enjoyed it. I hate working out. I do like being in shape, though. I wish I was one of the lucky ones who can just maintain their shape at all times, whether they work out or not. The lucky ones should be boiled in oil. We showered, and decided to have breakfast at the Bluebird Cafe on Prytania.

The Bluebird Cafe is one of the best diners in the city. It was about 10 o'clock when we got there. The air-conditioning was going full blast, which was a blessed relief. It was already about 90 degrees and about 90 percent humidity. It was going to be hotter than hell. After the waitress took our orders and left, I lit a cigarette. "Now, why do you think you need a detective?"

"You smoke?" Mike made a face, like he had just picked up a rock to find worms and slugs underneath it.

"Nasty habit, I know, but it's all I have left. No booze, no drugs, no fat, no sex with strangers. Just nicotine." Not completely true, but what did he know?

"Well, everyone should have some vices." He smiled at me and then stared down at the table. "This is kind of hard for me to talk about."

"It always is," I said in my most reassuring voice, one that I practiced for use on clients. I stared at his face, which was starting to redden a bit, and I wondered what he needed a detective for. Did he want me to spy on his lover to find out if he was cheating? Fidelity is an obsolete term these days. Guess what? If you think they're cheating, they are.

"I've lived here about two years." He took a deep gulp of his orange juice, and his hand was shaking just a little bit. "I moved here from Birmingham after I broke up with my boyfriend. There was no reason for me to stay there, you know? My family cut me off when I came out, my boyfriend was gone, and it's not like Birmingham is the most gay-friendly place. So I came to New Orleans and stayed."

Like thousands of others before you, I thought, as our waitress, Claire, delivered our food. He smiled at her, and she practically melted into a puddle in her shoes. She flirted with him for a little while, something about strawberry or grape jam, and he flirted right back at her. He was good at it. When she finally left, he looked at me and shrugged: *Women.*

I'm not ugly. I've had my share of waitresses and waiters flirt with me. But as far as Claire was concerned, I didn't exist. It was a humbling experience. I didn't like it. It would be hard to be friends with Mike Hansen.

"Well, after I moved here I started dating Ronnie Bishop. He's a mailman." He said it in the same tone that a priest might say the word heretic. "You know him?"

"Slightly," I said carefully. There was no sense in going into my own brief history with Ronnie. Who knew how he actually felt about the guy? Ronnie was a tall guy with a lean, muscled body and blond hair the color of white gold that rarely occurs in nature. He was good-looking, if you liked that type. I don't.

"We were together for two years, give or take." Mike kept talking as if I hadn't answered him. He still hadn't looked up from his food. "I don't want to bad-mouth him, but it wasn't fun."

"Why did you stay with him?"

"He threatened to kill himself every time I tried to leave." Mike shuddered. "It was awful. He was smothering and possessive and jealous. It got to the point that if I left the house to walk down to the A&P for a gallon of milk, he was sure I was meeting someone to cheat on him with. He would go into these jealous rages. After Mardi Gras this year, I asked him to move out. I couldn't take it anymore. I was gonna go crazy."

"Uh-huh."

"Well, he got mad and started yelling, calling me a whore and stuff like that." He took another swallow of orange juice. "He punched me in the face. I hit him back. My neighbor upstairs, Glen, called the police. I threatened to get a restraining order and have the police move him out. It was such a relief when he was finally gone."

Sad story, I was thinking as Claire came by and refilled my coffee.

"I have bad luck picking boyfriends, you know?" His voice got a faraway sound to it. "But I met this guy a couple of months ago when I was in Pensacola for the weekend."

Memorial Day weekend in Pensacola drew thousands of gay men from all over the country. Mike would fit right in with all the muscled studs packed into Speedos wandering the white sands. "Memorial Day?"

"No, I didn't go this year," Mike said. "Didn't feel like it. No, this was a few weeks earlier. I met a nice older guy at one of the bars there, and we went back to his hotel room." His eyes got dreamy. "The sex was incredible, and he was nice too. He told me he was from Savannah."

"OK." He didn't need a detective. He needed a travel agent.

"I couldn't stop thinking about him when I got back home," Mike said. "Crazy, I know, but I called Savannah information and couldn't get a listing for him."

"And you want me to find him for you?"

He laughed. "No, I found him myself. Here! He wasn't from Savannah at all. He'd lied about that. He was from here!"

I was confused. "Yeah?"

He lowered his voice. "It's kind of complicated. He's not out like we are. He has a wife and kids."

"I don't get it."

"I'm not finished." He rolled his eyes at me. "Anyway, he explained everything to me, about why he couldn't be out and everything. He comes from an old family here in the city, and his dad would have cut him off without a cent if he did. But his dad is sick, dying. Once he dies, he'll come out and divorce his wife, and we can be together."

It never ceased to amaze me how many married men in New Orleans are gay.

"So we started meeting in secret, because no one could know." Mike frowned. "But then, a week ago last Friday, he got a videotape in the mail at his office. Of us. Together in bed. The person who sent it wants money."

"Blackmail."

He nodded. "Exactly. He wants to just pay it and forget about it, but I don't think that's smart. I said we should hire a detective, and here I am." He leaned back in his chair, folding his arms.

I took a drink of my coffee and said nothing for a moment. "There are three ways to deal with a blackmailer, Mike. First, you can pay him. Second, you could go to the police and hope they'll be discreet. The third is to kill the blackmailer."

His face paled beneath the freckles. "I don't want you to kill anyone."

"Good." Like I would.

"And we can't go to the police—he's too well-known in town for that. People would talk, and it would get around."

"The only option left is to pay him."

"But if we do that, there's no guarantee that we'll ever be able to stop."

I shrugged. "And what do you want me to do?"

"Find him. Get all the copies of the tape." Mike smiled at me. "We'll pay you the $50,000 he wants. But that has to buy your silence too."

"I don't discuss my cases with anyone."

"Not even your lover?"

"Not even my lover."

"OK," Mike said. "You interested?"

Fifty thousand dollars was a lot of money. It was more than I made the last year. "Yeah."

"Great!" Mike smiled. "I'll go tell my boyfriend, and get some money for you as a deposit. You'll need to see the tape, I suppose. I'll have to get the note and tape from him. Do you want to meet me at my apartment around 2?"

"I'll type up a contract we can sign." I nodded.

He gave me his address. "I'll see you there at 2, OK?"

"OK."

"Just ring the bottom bell at the gate, and I'll come let you in." We shook hands, and he walked out. I sat there for a minute with my cooling coffee. I was at loose ends; Paul was out of town for a few days, and a nice little blackmail case could be fun. I wondered who Mike's closeted boyfriend was.

Fifty grand. I sat there for a minute, daydreaming about spending the money.

Claire slipped me the bill, and I had to laugh as I realized that Mike had stiffed me.

CHAPTER TWO

The temperature must have climbed by at least 10 degrees. The sun's brightness was blinding. I cursed myself for not having unpacked my sunglasses. They were still in my suitcase. I was drenched with sweat by the time the air-conditioning in my car started blowing cold air.

I had dealt with a blackmailer once before. I remembered my landlady's blackmail case. Someone had managed to get her on video having sex with a pair of hot young bodybuilders. Barbara hadn't been aware that they were both only 16. A lot of people would have crumbled in that situation and paid up. Not Barbara. She hired me. I caught the blackmailer and managed to get all of the evidence back.

This situation was not quite the same. I admit, it was hard for me to have any sympathy for Mike's lover. Selling yourself out for fear of being cut off from the cash is not exactly taking the high road. This guy had a wife and kids who were going to be hurt one day. I doubted the wife knew everything. Who was it that said the wife is always the last to know? However, I could put my own feelings aside. I wasn't being paid to preach morality to Mike or his lover. I was to be paid—quite well—to catch a blackmailer. There were lots of ways to spend $50,000. I'd just bite my tongue, not offer an opinion, and do my job.

And what kind of person was Mike Hansen? He was good-looking. He had a great body. Getting laid was not a problem for people like him. For him, it was a matter of who and when. He didn't seem very smart. The Mike Hansens of the world got away with below-average intelligence. They looked so good, they could get away with anything. It added to their appeal. How many times had someone told me that their ideal man was someone gorgeous but stupid? He didn't seem overly arrogant.

After a while wouldn't you get tired of looking at him? You can't stay in bed all day, no matter how much you want to. What did he talk about with his lovers after the sex was over? Weight lifting? Or did his lovers just lay there and bask in the glow? Sorry, I'd want more than that.

I pulled into the parking lot of my apartment building and let myself in the back door. My building was a turn-of-the-century Victorian originally built as a one-family dwelling. Now it was divided into six apartments. My apartment was one of the front two apartments on the first floor. I threw my gym bag on the bed and got a Dr. Pepper from the refrigerator. I had turned the air on that morning so the apartment was nice and cool. I hit the play button on my answering machine.

Beep. "Hey, honey. It's me, Paul. I just got into Newark and wanted to call and say I miss you. I have about an hour before my flight to Buffalo, so I think I am going to go grab a bagel or something. I'll call you tonight from Dallas."

Beep. "Chanse, where the fuck are you? Call me when you get in. I'm at the paper."

I grinned. That was Paige Tourneur, my best friend. A typical message. Paige hates talking into answering machines.

A crime reporter for the *Times-Picayune,* patience was not one of her virtues. I picked up the phone and called her direct line.

She answered on the second ring. "Tourneur." She sounded tired.

"Hey, girl."

"Oh, Chanse, thank God," she said. "I'm having a hell day today and was thinking about playing hooky this afternoon. Do you still have some of that killer weed we smoked the other day?"

"Yes." It was in a cigar box under my bed.

"Great. Do you want me to pick up some po'boys on the way over?"

"I can't today, Paige, at least not this afternoon. I have to see a client at 2 o'clock."

"Damn." She swore explosively. "I've got to get out of this pit, Chanse, I can't take it another minute today. You know what I'm writing up for tomorrow? A fucking 3-year-old was killed in a drive-by in Treme. A 3-year-old. They were trying to get his 12-year-old brother. What the fuck is wrong with this city? I need a goddamned cigarette." Paige's major beef with her job was not being allowed to smoke at her computer. For Paige, who smoked a pack and a half a day, this was major tragedy. "How the hell do they expect me to write this kind of crap and not be able to smoke at my desk? Bastards, bastards, bastards."

We met in college at LSU. I was a live-in brother at Beta Kappa fraternity. It surprises most people that I was a Greek in college. I got in because I was a football player. My background as trailer trash from East Texas wouldn't have gotten me a bid. I think it was because I was trailer trash that I sold my soul to the brotherhood. I wanted to get as far as possible from that double-wide on the hard dirt lot on the wrong side of Cottonwood Wells—not that there was a right side to that blot on the map—as far as possible from a drunken father who worked nights at the beef packing plant and always smelled of sour beer and stale blood, from a mother that rarely bothered to put on anything other than a blue fuzzy robe and drank gin all day, from the high school snots who looked down their noses at us.

My ability on the field soon started getting me invited to the "right" parties. I was always the worst-dressed boy. The girls sometimes managed to hide their smiles at my J.C. Penney's finest. Some of them wanted me to be their boyfriend, to be their date at dances and proms and birthday parties. I knew the only reason they'd be caught dead with me in public was because I was the football star. In their bitchy little society it was a status symbol to have me on their arm in my ill-fitting clothes. I hated them all, burning with a contained rage at their condescension, at the fact they thought they were doing me a "favor" by dating me. I took great pleasure in never touching them physically.

So when I was invited by Beta Kappa to pledge, I did. The brothers were the same kids from the right side of the tracks in Cottonwood Wells, but in Baton Rouge they didn't know about my father in the meat plant, working late nights and getting dried blood under his fingernails that never seemed to come off. They didn't know about my mother drinking her life away in a double-wide trailer, too drunk by 2 in the afternoon to keep up with *General Hospital.* They didn't know about the J. C. Penney's clothing that never fit me right. All they saw was the big guy with the football scholarship, which was something they could sell during future rush weeks. They never accepted me either. I was a trophy. By my third year in the house I hated them all. I stayed in my room, listening to music and studying. Sometimes I'd go out for a beer with a group of them. Much as I hated them, I liked wearing the sweatshirt with the BK on the front (even though I always thought of it as Burger King). I liked the big plantation-style house with the wide veranda, the big round columns, and the shady oak trees. The parties, fun at first, got old. I got tired of watching kids getting drunk and throwing up.

Paige was a lifesaver. I met her my third year in the house. That year the brothers were beginning to whisper about me. They wondered why I never seemed to get laid. They began to wonder why I wouldn't let anyone come with me to New Orleans. I was always afraid someone would see me in one of the gay bars there, my hand on some guy's ass and my tongue down his throat.

It was Little Sister Rush, which was an excuse to get drunk on Wednesday and Thursday as well as Friday. Some of the boys would fuck some poor drunk girl from the dorms and have something to brag about at Monday Night Meeting. It was Thursday night when I met Paige, International Drink Night at Beta Kappa. The party was held on the two upper floors of the house. Each room had a different drink. Everyone would move from room to room, getting more and more drunk. After an hour I went back down to my room, which was on the first floor. There was a girl sitting on my bed smoking a joint. Pink Floyd was playing on my stereo.

She blew out a stream of smoke. "Your room?"

I nodded.

"Sorry." She offered me the joint. "I had to get away from that crowd of idiots upstairs. The only way I could deal with them was to get high." She grinned. "You should lock your door."

I took a big hit and passed the joint back to her. It was spectacular grass. She was short, with reddish-blond hair and milky-white skin. She had a good figure, although a little on the plump side. She had large breasts that were barely contained within the red satin sleeveless blouse she was wearing. She had decent legs too. She was wearing a tight black skirt with fishnet stockings and black high heels. The most arresting feature about her was her eyes. The right one was blue, the left one green.

She took the joint from me. She inhaled, holding it in until she had to fight a cough. She blew the smoke out in a huge cloud, coughed a bit, and took a sip from a can of Diet Pepsi. "So, you're one of the brothers of Beta Kappa?"

"Yeah." I took the joint back from her. I was feeling pleasantly buzzed. "My name's Chanse."

"Take a chance, sing and dance." She giggled. "Paige Tourneur's my name, getting stoned is my game." She lit a cigarette. "So why did you join a fraternity? You don't seem like an asshole."

The automatic defense of the fraternity system rose to my lips. It was reflex. "It's like having 70 best friends." I made a face. "Right. Trying to forget that I'm just trailer trash from East Texas."

She nodded. "Makes sense."

"Why are you here?"

She shrugged. "Free booze. And research. I'm going to do a story about being a fraternity little sister for the school paper. I figured I could join up, get on the inside, and get the real story. Should be fascinating reading." She flicked her ash on the floor. "Don't know if I can go through with it now, though."

"Why not?"

"I don't think I could handle being around stupid people all of the time." She started laughing. "Every minute I spent upstairs, I felt my IQ slipping a point. It's like Caligula's court up there."

I started laughing. "Don't they wish! Everybody in this house has seen *Animal House* a few too many times. They're all busy trying to prove what studs they are—how many babes they can bag, how much booze they can drink. And the girls! I don't get them at all. Can't they see the guys are assholes?"

She smiled at me. "You're gay, aren't you?"

I had just taken a big hit off the joint and almost choked. "What?"

"Look, Chanse, don't pretend with me." She pointed her cigarette at me. "It's no good. I'm a little psychic, and I can tell. You're gay. Part of the reason you're here at Beta Kappa is you're hiding it."

What the hell, I thought. I was more than a little stoned. I didn't care if she printed it in the paper. "Yeah, yeah. I am."

"Secret's safe with me." She grinned at me. "Besides, I'll need an ally around here to keep all the other brothers' sweaty paws off my tits. We'll pretend we're a couple. What's it called? I'll be your beard."

So Paige became a Little Sister. We let everyone in the

house assume that we were a couple. We went to functions together and became good friends. At the end of the semester, she decided not to write the story after all. She kept on being a little sister. As much as she claimed to think the whole fraternity set up was just a bunch of "elitist bull-shit," I think she enjoyed being a part of it.

We remained close after I graduated. Once she got her degree in journalism, she took a job with the *TP* and moved to New Orleans. She started out working on the society pages. One night on her way home from work, she stopped at a convenience store to buy a loaf of bread and a pack of cigarettes. On impulse she decided to buy a can of Diet Coke and went back to the refrigerator cases. She dropped her purse. She bent down to pick it up, and while she was bent over, a 17-year-old kid whacked out on crack entered the store with a gun. He didn't see her, which was just as well, because he shot the clerk and cleaned out the register, scoring all of $37.29. Paige witnessed the entire thing. Her hands were still shaking when she sat down at her computer that night and wrote an editorial called "What Price Life?" The editorial was nominated for a Pulitzer. Her coverage of the kid's trial earned her a transfer to the crime desk. Everyone thought Paige was tough as nails. Only I knew that when she got home at night, she always lit a joint and had several drinks. Her dream was to become a novelist and leave the ugly sordid world of New Orleans crime behind her for good. It hadn't happened yet.

"Hang in there, baby. We can get good and stoned tonight," I said.

"So who's the new client?" Paige asked after allowing a low moan escape. "Anyone I know?"

"You know Mike Hansen?"

"The Coke delivery man? Great body? IQ of a snail?"

This city never ceased to amaze me. "How do you know him?"

"Are you kidding?" She laughed. "Twice a week he comes by here and fills the soda machines. Total babe. Every woman in the building—and a couple of the guys, I might add—always manage to be in the break rooms when he comes around. His Coke shirt is a size too small, and so are his shorts. He's packing quite a load in those shorts."

"Well, he's my new client."

She whistled. "Interesting. Too many women bothering him?"

"He's gay, Paige."

"Figures." She laughed again. "Rebecca over in Sports owes me dinner at Semolina's. What a sucker bet! She won't believe me when I tell her the good-looking ones with the great bodies that are over 25 and single are gay. So what's the problem?"

"I can't tell you that, you know."

"Until you need me to look something up in the morgue." Paige always exaggerates how often I need her to look things up for me. I don't ask her that often. "All right. Well, I'm going to duck out of here and head home and work on *Belle*." *Belle* was the romance novel she was working on, *The Belle of New Orleans*. "Call me when you're free, and I'll supply the po'boys."

"Deal." I yawned as she hung up. I walked back into the bedroom and looked at the packed suitcases sitting in the corner. I needed to unpack and do laundry. The unmade bed looked pretty inviting. My bedside clock read 11:15.

I could always do the laundry later, after I got back from meeting with Mike. I pulled my damp T-shirt over my head and slipped out of the shorts. I climbed back into the bed. The bed still carried a faint scent of Paul. I pulled the covers tightly around my body. I hated it when Paul went out of town. I lay there, relaxing, staring up at the ceiling and thinking about Paul.

I missed him. Much as I hated to admit it to myself, it was true. I closed my eyes and relaxed.

CHAPTER THREE

I must have fallen asleep.

The next thing I remember was a loud clap of thunder. I almost jumped out of my skin. It was so close the lightning must have struck almost right outside my bedroom window. All over the neighborhood car alarms were going off in an annoying chorus. I sat up in bed and glanced over at the clock on my nightstand: 2:24. I jumped out of bed and ran into the bathroom. Every muscle in my body ached from Mike's workout. I felt 100 years old. I turned on the spigot and brushed my teeth. I hate being late more than anything else. I always show up at parties or meetings 10 minutes early. I hate that whole "fashionably late" nonsense. Being late is rude. Since when is being rude in fashion?

I finished brushing my teeth and washed my face. My hair was a complete mess. Experience had taught me that running a brush through it would make it look worse. Since I was late, showering was out of the question. *Well, that's what baseball caps are for,* I reasoned. I grabbed one off my dresser, hurried into the living room, and picked up the phone book. I found Mike's listing and dialed. Busy. *He doesn't have call waiting?* I wondered as I pulled on a pair of jeans shorts. I dug through the dirty laundry for a T-shirt that wasn't stiff from dried sweat. I hate gadgets and modern technology as much as the next person, but even I have call waiting.

I went out the back door just as the rain started falling. The clouds looked more than threatening. They looked downright dangerous. Flash-flood weather. New Orleans is below sea level, and when a lot of rain comes down quickly the streets flood. I had gotten caught in a flash flood once. Five hundred bucks later my car was running again. I ran for the car, managing to get soaked by the time I got in. I gave the umbrella sitting in the back seat a dirty look as I started the engine. Huge drops of water were falling. My windshield wipers were doing double time trying to keep my line of vision free.

Driving in New Orleans at any time is an aggravation guaranteed to raise stress levels and blood pressure. No one uses turn signals. Delivery trucks frequently turn on their hazard lights and block a lane of traffic. The traffic signals are possessed by Satan. It is not unusual to pull up at an intersection where the light is both red and green at the same time. Several of the downtown streets are always being torn up. Negotiating all the one-way streets requires a degree in mapmaking. New Orleans is the only city I knew of where three one-way streets in a row all ran the same direction. Pedestrians ignore the traffic lights, walking out in front of a car without a second thought or glance. It's like living in a video game.

The streets were filling with water by the time I made it through the Central Business District. I was stopped at the light on Canal Street. It was looking more and more like a canal with every minute that passed. Cars went by throwing up sheets of water. All over the sidewalks people were ducking into doors for protection from the rain. It was dark enough to be night. Finally the light changed, and I crossed over into the Quarter. I swung to the left when I reached the cathedral and headed for Burgundy. The Quarter is a maze of one-way streets that always confuses the hell out of tourists, who make driving there a nightmare for locals. I turned right on Burgundy and, after I passed Dumaine, started looking for a parking spot. That's one thing they never get right in the television shows and movies that are filmed here. The hero can always find a parking spot right in front of where he has his business. The reality is you can drive around in circles forever trying to find a place to park.

My watch read a few minutes after 3 o'clock when I finally found a spot on St. Philip. The rain was still coming down by the gallon. I grabbed my umbrella, opened it and stepped out into the street. The water on St. Philip was up to my ankles. My shoes were completely soaked through. "Fuck," I muttered as I headed for the cover of the over-hanging balconies. I found Mike's building easily enough and rang the bell for his apartment. It wasn't one of those newfangled doorbells with an intercom so the person inside can find out who you are and then let you in. He was going to get wet coming out to let me in, but that's life. A few minutes passed, and I rang again. My umbrella wasn't protecting me much. My legs were getting wet. I was starting to get annoyed. I rang again. I debated going to use the pay phone on the corner. Then I noticed that the gate was ajar.

I pushed the gate open and stepped through it. The passage was too narrow for my umbrella. It was just a sidewalk with the main house right next to it on one side and the fence of the neighboring property on the other. The effect was very claustrophobic. The fence towered over my head and was lined with broken glass embedded in cement at the top. I briefly wondered how the hell Mike had ever gotten his furniture through the narrow passage. I closed my umbrella and swore again as I began to run to the courtyard behind the house. At the rear of the courtyard was a second building—probably slaves' quarters once—that had a flight of stairs going up to the second floor. The sidewalk continued around to the left of the building. I followed it and found the door to Mike's apartment. The door was all glass. I could see a spotlessly clean kitchen through it. As I knocked, the door swung open under my hand.

Goose bumps rose on my body. *Get out of here!* my instincts were screaming at me. *Something is very wrong here.* "Mike?" I called out as I stepped out of the water and into the kitchen. I was dripping water everywhere. The kitchen was white. Everything was in its place. The floor was black-and-white checkerboard tile beneath the growing puddle I was creating. There was water in one of the double sinks. In the rack dishes were dripping water. There was what appeared to be a protein shake in a glass on the counter. "Mike?" I called out, a little louder this time. There were two doors leading off the kitchen on either side. I glanced to the left and looked into the bathroom: empty. A wet towel was lying on the floor next to a pair of gray Calvin Klein boxers.

The other door led into what must be the living room. I could see an entertainment center against the wall. "Mike?" I walked through the door and stopped.

Mike was lying on his back, wearing only a pair of black jockey shorts. There was a growing puddle of blood underneath him. In that instant I saw an entry wound in the center of his chest. It looked almost like a third nipple. It was directly in line with the other two.

Thank God for police training. I was able to switch off human emotions and go right into police mode. I walked slowly over to him, not touching anything. I knelt down beside him and grabbed his wrist carefully. I felt for a pulse. The skin was still warm. Nothing. Just to be on the safe side, I felt for the artery in the neck. Again, nothing. His chest was not rising. He was dead.

OK, I have to get help, I thought, my umbrella dripping on the floor. *I can't use the phone here, I can't touch anything, I just have to get out of here without disturbing anything. No need for the paramedics, he's obviously dead.*

I turned and noticed the writing on the wall. It looked like it was written in blood. I walked over to it. The letters read FAGGOTS DIE. I got another chill. The blood was still wet, and droplets were trailing down from a few of the letters, streaks of blood on the white wall. I begin to shiver. *Oh, my God,* I thought, staring at the writing.

I had to get out of there. I was beginning to have trouble breathing. *Stay calm,* I told myself. My stomach was churning. It felt like I had swallowed acid. I leaned over and closed my eyes. "Deep breaths," I said over and over, trying to get my breathing under control, trying to calm the nausea I was feeling. Feeling somewhat better, I carefully walked out of the room, averting my eyes from the hateful writing and Mike's corpse. I walked outside. The downpour was easing up. There was no more thunder or lightning. I walked into the courtyard and looked upstairs. Lights were on. I climbed the steps, and knocked on the door. I heard footsteps. The door opened.

"Yeah?" The guy standing there wasn't wearing a shirt, only a pair of cutoff sweatpants. His brown hair was standing up in all directions, his eyes were hidden behind an ugly pair of glasses, and he hadn't shaved.

"I need to use your phone," I managed to say calmly, although I could feel that my teeth were starting to chatter. From the cold rain, I tried to convince myself, not from seeing a dead body. I had seen lots of dead bodies when I was a cop. I closed my eyes and took a deep breath.

"There's a pay phone at Matassas." He scowled. "How'd you get back here?"

"I need to use your phone," I said again. "Your downstairs neighbor has been shot."

He goggled at me. "What?"

I tried to control my temper. "Your downstairs neighbor has been shot, and I need to call the police and an ambulance."

"Mike?" He wasn't comprehending, so I pushed past him and walked over to the cordless phone that was lying on the counter. I picked it up and fumbled around in my wallet for a business card. Finding the one I wanted, I took another few breaths and dialed the number on the card.

"Mike's been shot?" He just stared at me. "Is he—"

"He's dead." I became aware of the odor of marijuana in the room. "And the police are going to be on their way soon, and they're going to want to question you, so I suggest you burn some incense or something."

"Mike's been shot." He walked into the kitchen, opened a drawer, and pulled out some incense sticks. He started lighting them, walking around his living room and placing them in holders. Once this was finished, he sat down on the couch and burst into tears.

Someone answered on the fifth ring. "Venus Casanova."

"Venus? Chanse MacLeod here. I need to report a body."

Venus was a police inspector who had been with the force almost 20 years. I knew her from my days as an officer. We weren't friends, but we got along OK. Every once in a while, we would get together for coffee or lunch. "You're sure?"

"He has a bullet hole in the center of his chest, and he isn't breathing. No pulse. Nothing. He looked pretty dead to me."

"Where are you?"

I gave her the address. "Call 911," she said and then added that she would get a car to come over immediately. "Hell, I might as well get over there myself. I guess you know a body when you see one." She hung up. I called 911. After the usual aggravation, I reported the shooting and that the police had already been notified.

I hung up the phone. The guy was still sobbing on the couch. *Great*, I thought. My teeth were still chattering. It was maybe 50 degrees in his apartment. He certainly believed in the benefits of air-conditioning. I was debating going outside to wait for the police when he stopped blubbering and looked at me. "Who are you anyway?"

"I'm Chanse MacLeod, and I had an appointment with Mike at 2 o'clock. I was late."

This seemed to satisfy him. He took off his glasses and wiped his face. "Man, I can't believe it. Mike's dead. Are you sure?"

"He looked dead to me, but I'm not a coroner." I moved toward the door. "I'm going to go outside and wait for the police."

"Yeah. Sure. Whatever."

I slipped back outside. The rain had stopped completely. The sun was out. The trees were still dripping. Hard to believe that just a little while earlier it has been pitch-black. I debated going back into Mike's apartment. Then I thought about the writing on the wall. I shivered again.

Maybe I could have saved him, I thought, as I sat down on the wet steps. If I hadn't made him wait, I might have been able to save him.

Or been killed myself as well.

Damn it all to hell.

I needed a cigarette. What the hell, maybe I had a few minutes. I walked out of the courtyard, leaving the gate ajar again, and hurried down Dauphine to Matassas Market. I bought a pack and a lighter. I lit one as I walked back. In the distance I could hear the sounds of sirens approaching. Thank God. I inhaled deeply as I walked back into the courtyard.

I forced myself to go back down that claustrophobic passageway and glance into Mike's living room through the window. I could see Mike's body lying there. It hadn't moved. I looked over to the left at the wall. Yes, the message was still there; it hadn't been a figment of my frightened imagination. Right next to a framed Herb Ritts print of a well-muscled and -oiled male nude.

FAGGOTS DIE.

I shivered again.

I heard a car screech to a halt in front of the building. I went back into the courtyard to wait for the police.

CHAPTER FOUR

Two uniformed officers came into the courtyard. I didn't recognize them. I introduced myself as the one who had called in and pointed them in the right direction. I walked over to the steps. They'd dried in the sun. It was getting hot again.

I went over several things in my mind. My client was dead. I knew that I shouldn't blame myself, but I couldn't help it. I fought against that nagging voice of guilt. I was an hour late. There was no way of knowing how long he'd been dead. And if I had arrived before the killer, then what? I can't stop a bullet. It was likely that I'd be dead too.

FAGGOTS DIE.

My God. I took some deep breaths to clear my head. A hate crime. A goddamned hate crime. It could've been me. It could've been someone I knew well. It could've been anyone. Some psychotic bigot decided to kill Mike as a lesson to faggots. I tried to remember the last gay hate crime in New Orleans. I couldn't.

Most of the natives pretty much had an attitude toward gays of "who cares." Maybe the society types might look down their noses at gays, but they didn't actively pursue oppression. New Orleans was an island of safety in the Deep South sea of bigotry against gays. Louisiana still had a sodomy law that was never enforced, as far as I know.

Gay friends in Birmingham once told me there were certain parts of town that they had to avoid for fear of their lives. The best treatment they could expect would be a bashing. When I heard that, I smugly thought about how safe I felt as a gay man in New Orleans.

Now I wasn't so sure anymore.

FAGGOTS DIE.

I had to get my emotions under control. Having a client killed out from under me was a new experience. It'd been a while since I'd seen a dead body. It was as awful as I remembered. The first time I had to deal with one on the force I'd thrown up. Maybe that was the reason that I left the force. When bodies stopped bothering me, it was time to get out.

My mind conjured up the picture of him lying there in his underwear, blood pooling underneath him. My teeth started to chatter again. I still felt cold.

FAGGOTS DIE.

I heard a door open. "You want some coffee?" the guy from upstairs asked.

"Yeah, that would be nice. Black, please." He brought out two cups. He handed me one. He'd put on a baseball cap.

"I can't believe he's dead," he said.

Someone I recognized came into the courtyard. "Believe it," I said, getting up.

Venus Casanova was in her late 40s but passed for 30. She had gone to the University of Tennessee on a basketball scholarship and now ran marathons and lifted weights to keep in shape. She was also the proud mother of two teenage daughters, both accomplished athletes. Venus was almost my height, and her looks always reminded me of some statuesque African deity. Her skin was the color of café au lait; her hair, black with reddish tints and trimmed close to her scalp. Despite the heat, she looked cool and professional in a yellow blazer, gray silk blouse, and matching wool skirt. "What's the story?" she asked me.

"Guy named Mike Hansen. He hired me this morning to look into something for him. We had an appointment this afternoon at 2, but I was late. I got here during the storm. The gate was open, so I let myself in when he didn't answer the bell. The door to his apartment was open, so I walked in and found the body." I gestured with my head in the direction of the apartment.

"Wait here." She turned her attention to the two patrol officers who had walked out of the apartment. She talked quietly to them and entered Mike's apartment.

I walked back over to the steps to wait. From experience, I knew it could be a while. I sipped the coffee. It was good. I said so.

"Thanks," the guy replied. He had put on a Saints T-shirt. "Mike hired you?"

"Yeah." I nodded. "I'm Chanse MacLeod, by the way."

"Glen Chandler." He shook my hand. "I can't believe this." He sighed. "We were supposed to go to a movie tonight."

"Were you dating?" I asked, curious.

He laughed. "We were just friends."

I looked at him. His glasses were kind of dorky-looking, but he was kind of cute. "What was his type?" I couldn't help it. I was curious.

He shrugged. "You know. Muscle boys, big and dumb. Just like him. Mike's perfect man was some big, dumb musclehead with a great job. Or family money." He laughed.

"My muscles aren't big enough, my job doesn't pay enough, and I've got a brain. Three strikes, I was out."

Venus came toward us. "Forensics are on their way," she said, pulling out a notebook and a pen. "Chanse, you want to go over the whole thing again from the beginning?" She looked at Glen. "And you are...?"

Glen stood up and offered his hand. "Glen Chandler. I live upstairs." He gestured toward his apartment door with his head. "Do you want some coffee?"

Venus shook her head. She was wearing dangly earrings with Egyptian symbols on them. "Mr. Chandler, do you mind waiting in your apartment? I'll have some questions for you, but I want to talk to Chanse first. Alone." Glen nodded and climbed up the stairs. We watched him walk up the stairs. His cutoff sweats were quite short. He had nice legs. "Cute," Venus said after the apartment door shut.

I shrugged. "What do you need, Venus?"

Venus flipped open a notebook and asked, "You say that the victim hired you this morning?"

"He approached me at the gym. He said that he wanted to hire me to check into something for him. We worked out together and then went to breakfast at the Bluebird Cafe."

"What did he want you to look into?"

Ordinarily, I don't discuss clients with anyone. This client was dead. Keeping my mouth shut wasn't doing him any good at this point. "He said his boyfriend was being black-mailed, and he wanted me to find out who was doing it."

"Blackmailed?" Venus scratched her head. "Who's the boyfriend?"

"Didn't tell me," I said. "He was going to this afternoon. He was going to show me the note and a videotape they sent."

"Why didn't he tell you who the boyfriend was right away?"

"Apparently, he's a closeted Uptown society type with a wife and kids and a father who would cut him off if he knew his son was really gay."

Venus sighed. "That narrows it down to how many?"

"Rhetorical, right?"

"Yeah," she said. "You see the writing on the wall?"

"Hard to miss."

"I don't know." She sat down next to me on the steps. "It looks like a hate crime, I have to say that. But it's weird, don't you think? He hires a P.I. in the morning. Hate-crime victim in the afternoon."

"Coincidence?"

"I don't like coincidences." She was about to say something else, but loud voices coming from the direction of the gate interrupted her. We headed over there.

A man in a navy-blue suit was hassling a patrol officer stationed at the gate to keep people from coming in. "I'm telling you, you fascist Nazi, that I have to get in there," the man yelled. "I've an appointment, and I don't care what your orders are!"

"What's going on here?" Venus growled.

The man turned his attention to her. I recognized him and inwardly groaned. It was Jarrett Phillips, professional gay activist. He ran an organization called Gay Rights Now! in the Faubourg Marigny. He was a shade under six feet tall and sported a nice tan. His white-blond hair was starting to thin. His blue eyes narrowed as he looked at Venus, and his scowl faded. A smile warmed up his face. He looked like a used car salesman. His tone sounded like someone about to sell you a car with an engine that might hold together for another 100 miles—if you're lucky.

"Jarrett Phillips." He stuck his hand out.

"Venus Casanova. I'm in charge here, Mr. Phillips. How can I help you?" Her voice was pleasant with an edge to it. Venus was not someone to fuck with.

"If you could tell this gestapo agent to let me by, I'd greatly appreciate it."

She shook her head. "I'm afraid that's not possible, Mr. Phillips—"

"Jarrett."

She continued as if he'd said nothing, "This is a crime scene. Until I'm satisfied, no one goes back there who's not part of my investigation. Understood?" There was iron in her voice.

"I have an appointment with Mike Hansen. It's very important—"

That's weird, I thought. *He's not curious about the crime scene.*

"I hate to break this to you, Mr. Phillips, but Mike Hansen is deceased."

He looked at her for a moment. His mouth opened and closed, opened and closed. He noticed me for the first time. "Chase, right?"

"Chanse."

"Is this true?" His voice was barely above a whisper. I nodded at him and lowered my eyes. "But we had an appointment!"

How inconvenient of Mike to get killed, I thought.

I didn't like Jarrett Phillips. I had met him once at a party. He pigeonholed me in a corner of the room, bombarding me with facts and figures. He kept poking me in the chest with a finger. When he finally figured out that I was not able to donate vast amounts of money to his organization, he moved on. It was just in the nick of time. One more poke of his finger in my chest would have cost him a tooth or two. I had a slight bruise when I got home that night. He poked me each time in the exact same place.

Venus walked him away from the gate. She was talking quietly. Every so often he would nod. Finally, they exchanged business cards, and he walked away. He walked as if someone had kicked him in the balls. I wonder if it was what Venus said to him that did it—or was it the screwing up of his schedule?

Venus walked back over to me. "Chanse, I have to ask you to promise me something."

"What?"

"Promise me you won't say anything to anyone about the graffiti in the living room. I don't want anyone to know this may be a hate crime, OK?"

I stared at her. "Venus, I can't promise that."

Her eyebrows came together. Her voice was silky. "Why not?"

"I think it's wrong," I said. "It looks like a hate crime. Maybe it's not. But not letting anyone know that there may be some crazy out there killing gay men, just for being gay..." I shook my head. "Venus, people have to know to be careful."

"Damn it, Chanse, we don't know for a fact this is a hate crime." Her voice rose. She pulled me into the passageway to the back. "There's no sense in having a public panic."

"And what if there's another one?" I was starting to get

mad. "Are you prepared to live with that, Venus? I'm not. What if it's someone I care about next time? Someone you care about?" This was a veiled reference to the rumor around the force that Venus was a closeted lesbian. I didn't think she was. I thought it was a typical knee-jerk white straight-male reaction to a tough, powerful woman—"Hey, she's got to be a lesbian." Ordinarily, I wouldn't say anything like that to Venus. I don't know her that well, but I respect her.

"You saying that I don't care about gays?"

"Maybe you just don't understand what it's like."

"Fuck you, Chanse." She started laughing. "Get the fuck off of your soapbox, OK? Look who you're talking to. I'm a black woman, for God's sake—you think I don't know about prejudice?"

I grinned back at her.

"Just at first, that's all I'm asking, OK?"

"Yeah, OK." I shook my head. "But if there's another one before you go public, I'm telling everyone that you kept it quiet. Got it?"

"Fair enough." We shook hands solemnly. "Do you think the matter he hired you for might have something to do with this?"

"Doesn't make much sense." I thought about it. "He wasn't the one with the money. And why kill the pigeon?"

She shrugged. "Intimidation? Look, I killed your squeeze, pay up."

"Well, if people started dying around me, I'd go straight to the police."

"Didn't Mike, sort of? He hired a private eye. Maybe the blackmailer didn't think that was a hot idea."

We walked into the courtyard. I shrugged. "I don't know, Venus. I just don't know. Anyway, it's not my problem. It's in your hands now."

"You're not curious?"

"I don't do murders, Venus. If I wanted that, I could have stayed on the force." Glen was still sitting on the steps. Mike's body was being wheeled out on a gurney. They had trouble making it out the door and turning. *How did he get his furniture in there?* I wondered again. Glen's face turned white as they brought the body out. He looked away.

"I need you to come in and make a statement. What's good for you?" Venus watched the gurney go by.

"I can do it now. My car is parked on St. Philip, though. I might get a ticket."

"Give it to me. But it better be from today."

She went to talk to the photographer. I walked back over to the steps and sat down. "You doing OK?" Glen looked kind of greenish.

He nodded. "I can't believe he's actually dead."

"Did you know him well?"

"Yeah." He sipped his coffee, made a face, and poured it out into the flower bed next to the stairs. "We were close. He always told me I was his best friend."

"I'm sorry."

"Don't be." He gave a kind of half laugh. "I didn't like him that much. I mean, he could be sweet sometimes, but he could be the most selfish asshole. Sometimes I just wanted to punch that pretty face. I put up with his shit because I thought maybe someday he would change his mind about me."

"You were in love with him?"

He looked at me. "I just wanted to sleep with him. He thought I was in love. A relationship between us wouldn't have ever worked. I wasn't that crazy." He looked at his hands. "And now he's dead." He looked up. Venus was walking over to us.

"Mr. Chandler, I need to ask you some questions."

He looked at me instead of her. It pissed Venus off. He was one of those men who always assumed that the man was in charge. "Why?"

"Standard procedure." Venus flipped her notebook again. "I'll see you at the station, Chanse," she went on, dismissing me.

I walked out and sighed. I lit another cigarette. Paul wouldn't be back for four days. I'd get the smell off me by then.

CHAPTER FIVE

It was almost 7 o'clock by the time I got home. Paige was smoking a cigarette on the front steps. She had a paper sack holding our dinner with her. I'd called her from the police station when I was finally done telling my story. I was tired and feeling bitchy. I was starving. Once the initial shock had worn off, my appetite had kicked back into gear. Paige waved at me as I drove past and parked.

"Exciting day, huh?" she stubbed out her cigarette on the brick steps as I walked up to her. "You don't find a body every day."

"And that's just fine with me." I unlocked the door, and we stepped inside. I walked over to the answering machine. No messages. It would have been nice to hear Paul's voice. I grabbed a can of Dr. Pepper for myself and a diet Coke for Paige. I walked back into the living room. She was emptying the sack onto the coffee table. The aroma of deep-fried shrimp filled the room. I love shrimp po'boys. My stomach growled.

Paige took a huge bite out of hers. "Do the cops think you're a suspect?"

"Who knows what they think." I switched on the television. "I found the body. Usually, whoever reports it is the killer. They kept me down there long enough."

"That sucks." Paige popped a handful of chips in her mouth. "Why did Mr. Coca-Cola delivery man want to hire you?"

"He said his lover was being blackmailed," I said. "He wanted to put a stop to it."

"Why didn't the boyfriend hire you?" She popped the last bite of her sandwich into her mouth. She sighed. She loved her po'boys. "You gonna look into it?"

"Why?" I finished mine.

"Clear your name and all that shit."

I gave her what I hoped was a withering glance. "This isn't a TV show, darlin'. That's the cops' job."

"Like they give a shit when a fag is killed." Paige lit up a cigarette.

"Venus is in charge of the case."

Paige blew smoke at the ceiling. "Well, well. A dyke in charge? Maybe something will get done then."

"Venus isn't a dyke."

"Whatever." She reached for the red box sitting on the end table and pulled out the plastic bag of pot and the pipe. She took a long hit and held it in. She passed me the pipe.

"Just because she played basketball in college doesn't make her a dyke." I took a hit.

"Well, odds are in favor," Paige said.

"You covering this for the paper?"

"They offered it to me but I turned it down."

"Why?"

She smiled at me lazily. "Dumb ass, you fucking found the body. My best friend. That's a conflict for my journalistic integrity."

"Never stopped you before."

"True." She passed the pipe back to me. "But they wouldn't let me cover it the way I'd want to. I mean, aren't you tired of how the cops just blow off gay crimes?"

"I wasn't aware that they did."

"What?" She stared at me. "Babe, someone could fire-bomb Lafitte's during it's busiest time, and they'd never find who did it. Hell, they wouldn't look very hard. Do you honestly not know how many hate crimes against gays there are in this city?"

I shrugged. I hadn't thought about it much. I pretty much did whatever I wanted, and nothing ever happened to me. Every once in a great while a truckload of rednecks might drive by and scream "Faggot!" at me, but other than that...

FAGGOTS DIE.

"At least one bashing a week." She lit another cigarette. "And in the Quarter, of all places, where the gay tourist dollar brings in millions to the city yearly." She was off and running now. "Everyone thinks of New Orleans and the French Quarter as a gay Mecca, a place where gays can come and be openly gay and be safe. New Orleans doesn't care who or what you are, right? Wrong, wrong, fucking wrong. How many times do the cops raid the gay bars? At least once or twice a year."

"Wow."

"How can you not give a shit?" She stabbed the air with her cigarette. "Do you know how many unsolved gay murders there are in this town? Do you?"

"No."

"More than you'd think. And many times when the killers are caught, they get off. All they have to do is say,

'Oh, he made a pass at me,' and a jury will let them off." She sat back, wound down from her tirade. "It's getting better, though. Much as I hate to admit it, that asshole Jarrett Phillips is getting a lot done."

Him again. "There's a lot of crime in general in town, not just gay ones."

"Ain't that the fucking truth." She picked up a stray shrimp off the wrapper of my sandwich. She chewed on it. "Aren't you the least bit curious about who killed your client?"

"Not right now," I shuddered. *FAGGOTS DIE.* "I don't do murders, Paige. That's for the police."

"Used to be a cop, din'tcha?"

"Used to be." I picked up the garbage from our meal and shoved it into the bag. "Not anymore. I trust Venus. She's a good cop."

My doorbell rang, followed by frantic pounding. "Open up! It's the police!"

"Oh, fuck!" Paige tossed the pipe and the bag into the red box, shut it, and shoved it under a sofa cushion.

I laughed. I felt pleasantly relaxed. "Don't you recognize Blaine's voice by now?" I opened the door. "Asshole, you scared Paige out of her panties."

Blaine threw his arms around me and reached up to kiss my cheek. His green eyes were wide open and innocent-looking. "Sorry, Paige," he said meekly. Blaine was an old friend from my police academy days. He lived with his lover, Todd Laborde, in a beautiful Greek Revival house on the other side of the park.

"You are such a fuck, Blaine." Paige reopened the box and reloaded the pipe. She was not overly fond of Blaine.

He teased her too much. He had also fixed her up with his brother Ryan, who at the time had been fresh out of a divorce. Paige swore it would take her until she was 50 to forgive Blaine for that.

He winked at me. "Ryan's latest just dumped him. Wanna give him a second chance?"

Paige held the smoke in for a long time and then blew it at him. "Only if he's had a full frontal lobotomy."

"Jesus, Paige!" He stepped back out of the cloud of smoke. "I'm in uniform!"

Blaine was still a wearing member of New Orleans' finest. Police uniforms look good on very few cops. Blaine was one of the exceptions. Paige believed that he had them tailored to fit him like a body stocking.

Blaine and I had met at the academy. After we had joined the force, I ran into him one night dancing at Oz. He was wearing a black ribbed tank top that was about a size too small and a pair of white jeans cut off just below the curve of his ass. He grinned at me. "I'm working undercover," he shouted into my ear above a then-current Madonna dance hit. "Working on getting under the covers with this one!" He jerked his thumb at some shirtless, sweaty boy with pecs the size of grapefruits. I laughed, and we became friends.

Paige smiled at Blaine and offered him the pipe. "On duty?"

"Off." He took a hit and passed it to me. "One day I'm going to pick up the paper and read a story with your byline about drug use on the force, aren't I? And the first sentence will be 'I've gotten stoned with Office Blaine Tujague more times than I can remember.' And then I'm going to be royally fucked."

"Like anyone in New Orleans would give a shit." Paige took the pipe back from me.

Blaine turned to me. "Had some excitement in the Quarter today, huh?"

"Yeah."

"Venus called me." He took another hit. "She doesn't really consider you a suspect."

"That's nice."

"Didn't find the murder weapon either." He looked at me. "Got anything to drink?"

I got him a beer. He took a long drink. "Paige, none of this shit is for the paper, OK?"

"Not even my story," she said with a wave of her hand.

"OK, then." He took another drink. "He was shot once in the chest. The bullet severed an artery and nicked his heart, which stopped immediately. No forcible entry into the apartment. No murder weapon. Don't have an estimated time of death yet."

"Well, it was sometime between when he left the Bluebird and when I got there."

Blaine looked at me. "Anyway, they didn't find any evidence of a blackmailer."

"What?" I stared at Blaine. Paige was leaning forward on the love seat. She was stoned but alert.

"Venus had them scour the place looking for the letter and tape you told her about." He whistled. "Not a thing. Didn't look good for you for a while there, old buddy."

That explained why they'd kept me at the station for so long. "So why did they let me go? Why am I not a suspect?"

"Still are. You know Venus," Blaine said. "Just not a primary, that's all. Your story didn't check out."

"Maybe the killer took the evidence." Paige lit a cigarette. "I mean, maybe the blackmailer and the killer are the same person. Why wouldn't he take the evidence?"

"The place hadn't been searched. How did the killer know that the evidence was even there?"

"The killer was someone who knew him," I theorized. "Someone who had been inside the apartment before. No forcible entry, right? Mike let his killer in. And if the killer took the blackmail evidence, it's pretty reasonable to assume that the killer was also the blackmailer. And since this person knew Mike, had been inside his place before, he didn't have to search. He knew where the stuff was."

"Bingo." Blaine took another hit. "Jeez, but this is some killer shit, Chanse."

"I bought it, I didn't grow it." My mind, despite the effects of the pot, was racing. "Did anybody see anything?"

"The only thing anybody saw was what saved your ass." Blaine smiled at me. "Someone across the street saw you go in the gate about five minutes before you called it in. Venus figures you didn't have time to kill him, dispose of the tapes and the weapon, and then call it in. She's not ruling you out, though."

"Nice of her, I'll send her a card."

"You guys are assuming that there actually was a black-mailer," Paige said.

We looked at her. She rolled her eyes. "You only have Mike's word there was a blackmailer. You don't even know if there was a boyfriend. You sure don't know his name. No evidence, right?"

"Then why would he hire me?"

"Don't know." She stood. "I gotta run. Early morning

tomorrow." She kissed me on the cheek. "Call me and let me know how you're doing, OK?" I nodded. She let herself out.

"She's right." Blaine put his hand on my leg. "He could have made the whole thing up."

I looked at his hand. Blaine and his lover, Todd Laborde, had an open relationship. Occasionally, Blaine and I had slept together. It had never meant anything, just sexual release. We hadn't done it in over a year. Blaine said that Todd didn't care about his activity outside their "marriage," but Todd had never been overly friendly to me. Just polite. "Todd out of town?" I asked.

"Uh-huh." He started rubbing the inside of my leg.

"Blaine, not a good idea."

"Why not?"

"Paul for one." I didn't want to admit I was also shaken up about finding the body.

"He's gone too, and you don't know what he does when he's out of town."

"No."

"OK." Blaine stood and stretched lazily. He walked to the door, where he gave me another hug and kiss. "Oh, they found a trick book."

"A what?"

"An address book. You know, where you keep the phone numbers of your tricks?"

I knew what he meant. Straight men called them little black books. Gay shops sold them, and they had TRICKS embossed in gold leaf on the covers. "Yeah?"

Blaine grinned. "Mike Hansen was a busy little boy."

"Venus doesn't think it was a hate crime?"

"No." He scratched his head. "It's the damnedest thing, Chanse. I mean, I saw the crime-scene photos, and my guts just clenched up. But it's weird. Most hate crimes are bashings that get out of hand and the victim dies, you know? This looked planned. That's why Venus isn't sure."

I shut the door behind him. It was a little after 10 o'clock. Paul's last flight arrived in Chicago at 9, and he was supposed to call me when he arrived. *There could have been a delay,* I thought. *Any number of things.* I walked into the bedroom and undressed. *"You don't know what he does when he's out of town."* I got under the covers. I set my alarm. I stared at the ceiling, wondering what Paul was doing in Chicago. I closed my eyes.

FAGGOTS DIE.

Most hate crimes aren't thought out in advance. I opened my eyes. *Maybe this is a psycho with a brain.*

Comforting thought.

CHAPTER SIX

I am not a morning person.

When the alarm went off at 8 A.M., I sat up in bed and glared at it. I debated going back to sleep. I didn't have any reason to get up. No client. I could lie in bed all day if I wanted and who'd care? With a groan I got up. I rubbed my eyes and walked into the kitchen. I started a pot of coffee.

I hadn't slept well. I hadn't expected to. The years I'd been a cop had hardened me to death, blood, and violence. Since going on my own, though, I hadn't stumbled on a corpse. I dreamed about murder all night. Sometimes I was the victim. Other times it was someone I knew and cared about: Blaine, his lover, or Paul. In every dream I saw a finger dipped in blood writing *FAGGOTS DIE* on the wall. My whole body still ached from that grueling workout. I tried to loosen up some of my tightened muscles. Weird that the person responsible for this was dead. I sighed. *Murder: that wasn't what I left the force for.* My P.I. practice consisted mainly of checking out insurance fraud, spying on adulterous spouses, background checks, and designing security systems.

And here I was mixed up in a murder.

I was confident that Venus Casanova wouldn't just brush Mike's murder under the rug. She was a good cop, tough and tenacious. She wouldn't care if Mike was a pedophile who'd molested her own daughter. If it was her case, she wouldn't rest until she'd covered every base. She wasn't the type to sit around waiting for an anonymous tip. She'd make sure something happened.

I poured a mug of coffee and sat in the living room. I reached for a pack of cigarettes. I lit one and inhaled. How can something that feels so good be fatal? I turned on the television and flipped through the channels. Nothing. Must've sucked in the old days when there were just three channels with nothing worth watching as opposed to the mess cable provided now.

I pulled on a pair of baggy workout shorts and a tank top. I'd set the alarm to go to the gym—might as well go. I was so sore, I wasn't sure I could dress myself. I decided that if I could, the gym was an option. "No pain, no gain," I told myself, finishing a second cup. I've always hated that phrase. Whenever some grinning moron said that to me, I wanted to punch him. It made me think of a gym teacher named Coach Billings. Coach Billings didn't coach a sport. He was the strength trainer for all sports, and the jocks at Cottonwood Wells High had to work out under his watchful eyes. He lifted weights himself like an addict. I can remember struggling with a bench press. It was the third set, I needed to do eight reps, and after four it was getting heavy. By the fifth, I knew I was going to lose it. It was going to crash down onto my chest. Coach Billings saw me struggle and pushed spotter aside. He started screaming at me. Spittle flew in my face. I managed to finish the set. I sat up on the bench, and he smacked me on the back. "No pain, no gain," he smirked into my face.

If I'd had the strength to lift my arms, he'd have lost a few teeth that day.

There was no one in Bodytech when I arrived. I nodded at Alan, who was chewing on a bagel at the front desk. He swallowed. "Sucks about Mike Hansen, huh?"

I stopped. "Yeah."

"In the paper this morning." He tapped it with his bagel. "Said you found him. Drag."

"Yeah. A drag."

"So who do you think offed him?"

"No clue."

Alan laughed. "It would suck to have that case, I gotta say." He looked even more chipmunkish than usual this morning. It was the cheeks full of half-chewed bagel.

"Why?"

"Come on, Chanse." His blue eyes opened wide. "You're joking."

I shrugged. "No, I'm not."

"Everybody hated that prick." Alan shook his head. "You need to get out more."

"I didn't hate him."

"Then you didn't know him."

"I didn't." I waited. I knew Alan. He was anxious to gossip.

"Well..." he looked around, even though we were the only people in the gym. "The first person I'd check out is the ex."

"Ronnie Bishop?"

"He had it bad." Alan shook his head. "I invited them to a party last year. It was sick, watching the two of them together. Ronnie waited on him hand and foot. The whole time Mike was working the room. The shit even put the make on Greg."

I raised my eyebrows. "Really?"

Alan made a face. "Can you believe his fucking nerve? In my house, he makes a play for my partner. He thought he could have anyone."

"And Ronnie knew?"

"He was oblivious. I mean, everyone knew that Mike had been cheating from day one. Ronnie refused to believe it. He was like a puppy dog, jumping every time Mike snapped his fingers, hoping to get petted."

"How did he take it when Mike left him?"

Allen rolled his eyes. "Pitiful. He'd start crying during his workouts. Not eating, not sleeping. Pitiful."

I nodded. "Sad."

"Justin Warren hated him too," Alan went on. "I had to take him into my office one day. He was screaming at Mike. I thought he was going to throw weights or something. All I need." He shook his head. "All those mirrors. Jeez, that would've been a mess."

"Justin Warren? As in the Deveraux-Warrens?"

Alan nodded. "That's him."

Interesting. Justin Warren and Remy Deveraux had been together for years. "What did Justin have against him?"

"Ask him," He said. "No idea."

"Thanks, Alan." I walked away.

I started my workout. I kept thinking about Mike. He'd seemed like a nice guy. Alan hadn't liked him much. If he was to be believed, no one did. This Justin Warren situation was interesting. I knew Justin and Remy slightly. I'd never been invited to their parties. That was fine. I'm not one of those queens who gets offended when left off a guest list. I don't like parties. I'm not comfortable at them and only go when I'm dragged. Parties are a waste of money and time. Besides, that's what bars are for. In New Orleans, that's heresy. The city revolves around its social niceties. Who you are is defined by whose parties you go to, and who comes to yours.

Once I had finished my workout, I sat in the hot tub, positioning my body in front of the jets so I could work the tightness out. I wished I could have my own hot tub. After cleaning up, I went home, thinking about Justin Warren along the way. *How had he known Mike?* I thought it hardly possible that Mike had been one of Justin and Remy's friends. He had been just a Coca-Cola delivery driver. Maybe they had invited Mike to their parties as a decoration. He'd have been easy on the eyes.

There were three messages on my machine when I got home.

Beep. "Chanse, it's Paul. I'm in Minneapolis now. Sorry I didn't call you last night, but the flight was two hours late, and I didn't want to wake you up. Plus I was tired. Apparently, you had to present asshole papers to be allowed as a passenger on that flight. I'll be in Boston tonight and will call you. I miss you."

Beep. "Hey, babe. Paige here. Guess who got reassigned to your client's murder? Apparently, Jarrett Phillips is making a stink about this, and he wants swift justice for poor Mike Hansen. Since Jarrett the prick doesn't scare me, they put me on it. Want to give me an exclusive? Ha-ha-ha. I just spent an hour listening to him rant and rave about how the cops and the paper don't care about gays. I almost told him there's just one gay we don't care about—being him. Why didn't the killer do us all a favor and kill Jarrett? I shouldn't say that, because someday when someone does whack his sorry ass, I'll be a suspect. Call me when you get in, OK, babe?"

Sucks to be you, I thought.

Beep. "Um, hi, Chanse. This is Glen Chandler. Um, you know, Mike's upstairs neighbor. We, um, met yesterday? I hope you, um, don't mind, but I looked you up in the phone book. Would you mind giving me a call? Maybe we could, um, meet for coffee or something." He then left his number. I wrote it down. Interesting. I wonder what he wants? I picked up the phone and called Paige at the paper.

"Tourneur."

"Are you naked?" I said, lowering my voice.

"Yep, nipples to the wind." She giggled. "Thanks, I needed an obscene phone call. What a shitty fucking day."

"How come you wound up with the story?"

"Because I did that interview with Jarrett Phillips when he opened up his office." She sighed. "Smarmy bastard. I've got to go over there this afternoon to talk to him about 'the implications of the murder.'"

"What implications?"

"His words, not mine." She was making smacking noises. Very annoying.

"You chewing gum?"

"Some idiot told me to try it since I can't smoke at my desk." She made a spitting noise. "There. In the trash where it belongs. Like gum works. Why, oh why, must they torture me this way?"

"Any new leads?"

"Venus isn't talking. Big shock there," she said. "I do not want to meet Jarrett Phillips. I'd rather have my vulva tattooed and pierced. I must've built up a shitload of bad karma in a past life. And I have to go to a gallery opening tonight. Wanna come?"

"Who's the artist?"

"Who knows? Someone who probably couldn't draw a straight line along a ruler and throws paint on canvas. Art. Free champagne and food, though," she said. "Please come. You owe me."

"How you figure that?"

"Because I'm your very best friend in the world. Come on, it'll be fun. We can get stoned and make fun of everyone."

I considered. Art openings are fun when you're with Paige and stoned. I don't know much about art, but she does. Get a few glasses of champagne in her, and she doesn't care whom she offends. Not that she ever cares. "OK."

"I'll pick you up at 8."

"Great."

"I don't suppose I could talk you into coming with me to see Jarrett Phillips?" Her voice took on a wheedling tone.

"I don't see why you have to talk to him in the first place."

"Mike sometimes volunteered for him. He thinks the murder was directed at his group."

Uh-oh, I thought. *FAGGOTS DIE.* "Does he want to share with you his grassy knoll theory as well?"

That made her laugh. Paige's theory on the JFK assassination was that Marilyn Monroe was behind it. She'd written a long essay on the subject, fabricating all of her evidence, and considered selling it to a tabloid. It was quite funny. A tabloid would've probably run it. "I'll see you at 8," she said.

I hung up, and looked at Glen Chandler's phone number. *What could he want?* I wondered. I dialed. I was about to hang up when someone answered. "Hello?"

"Chanse MacLeod."

"Chanse?"

"Yep."

"Thanks for calling me back!"

"What's up?"

"I was wondering…" he paused. "Would you meet me for coffee sometime?"

"Sure." What was this all about? "Free this afternoon, as a matter of fact."

"Really?" I could almost see his smile. "How about 3 o'clock at Kaldi's?"

"See you there," I said and hung up the phone.

What Alan said made me curious. Why was Justin Warren so pissed at Mike? How had their paths crossed? And why did Glen Chandler want me to meet me for coffee? It didn't make sense. I'd like to think that Glen had been swept away by my good looks. Somehow I thought there was more to it than that. I'm not Quasimodo, but pretty boys don't line up at my door with their tongues hanging out of their mouths. It must have something to do with Mike's murder.

I looked at my watch: 11 o'clock. I had time for a short nap. Maybe I could have a chat with Justin and Remy. It wouldn't hurt to ask them a few questions. I'm sure Venus was busy. Besides, it probably was nothing. Just satisfying a little curiosity, that's all.

I got into bed. I hate when my bed is empty. I missed Paul more than I cared to admit. Maybe this is getting serious for me.

CHAPTER SEVEN

Despite the heat, the lower Quarter was alive with people. I could feel the sweat rising to the surface of my skin. I passed a tour group. They all looked like they were going to have heatstroke. Some were fanning themselves. Others were sipping water. The tour guide was talking about one of the houses. I listened to her as I walked by. It was fascinating. She was talking about how the original occupant of the house had tortured her slaves. Too bad it was the wrong house. Her group looked enthralled. I got to the corner at Chartres.

The sound of a jazz band playing "When The Saints Go Marching In" drifted down Chartres from Jackson Square. There's always music playing down there. Some of the street bands are better than those with recording contracts. New Orleans is a city of great music. I debated wandering down there for a minute or two. I love Jackson Square, even in the heat. The street artists and fortune-tellers would be out, umbrellas blocking the sun. There'd be mimes with melting make up. I looked at my watch and decided against it. I hadn't hung out in the Square in a long time. I decided that I'd have to make time for it soon.

I headed down the final block to the corner of Decatur and St. Philip. A jazz band was playing in the restaurant on the other side of Decatur. I listened to them for a while.

Some young African-American kids with taps on their Reeboks were dancing for change. I pushed open the door to Kaldi's.

Glen was sitting at a window seat. He had shaved and gotten rid of the glasses, and he was wearing a backwards-turned baseball cap. I wouldn't have recognized him if he hadn't stood up and called my name.

I walked over. The table was covered with paper. "Let me get a drink."

He nodded.

I ordered a cup of steaming hot dark roast. The girl at the counter looked at me like I was nuts. I looked at her. Her hair was dyed black. Her nose and eyebrow were pierced. She had spider webs tattooed on the webbing between her thumb and forefinger on both hands. *So I like hot coffee instead of body mutilation. Sue me.*

"Hot coffee?" Glen raised an eyebrow when I sat down with him. He'd moved some of the paper so I could sit down.

I shrugged. "I like hot coffee."

He grinned. His face lit up when he smiled. He had large brown eyes that I hadn't noticed. "A gazillion degrees outside and humid as hell, and you drink hot coffee."

"I don't let the weather decide what I eat and drink."

He smiled. "Can I use that sometime?"

"Huh?"

He gestured at all the paper. "I'm a writer. I don't know how I'll use it, but someday it'll fit into something."

"Published anything?"

"No," He said. He started stacking the papers neatly. "I'm writing a book."

"About?"

"Gay life here." He lit a cigarette, a long thin brown one. "It's kind of trashy."

That could be fun. I said so.

"I think so. Obviously. Otherwise I wouldn't be writing it." He took a long drag. I wished I had one. "New Orleans has been almost completely ignored in gay literature—can you believe it? Lots of books have been written in and about New Orleans, but never one about gay men."

"Weird."

"It's true." He flicked ash into a chipped black plastic ashtray. "It amazes me. This city amazes me."

"Yeah." I stared at his cigarette. It looked so good, I could almost feel the filter on my lips, taste the nicotine in my mouth, the feel of the smoke….

"Do you want one?" He'd noticed my lust. He offered me the pack. "Or are you trying to quit?"

"Not hard." I took one from him and lit it. It was menthol. I didn't care. "So what's the book about?"

"You really wanna know?"

"Yeah."

"Well, it's called *The World Is Full Of Ex-Lovers.*" He smiled. "It's about four gay men who live in the Quarter around a courtyard. It begins when one of the guys, who's the main character, moves here from Topeka. He's only 23, been out of college for a year, and just broke up with his lover. He decides he wants to get out of Kansas—"

"Can't imagine why."

"And moves here. He gets an apartment in the Quarter and goes to work for a gay newspaper. Before long, he becomes friends with his three neighbors, and it's about how they live—the bars, drugs, love, romance, one-night stands, all of that."

"What about AIDS?"

"That's a tough one." He lit another cigarette from the butt of the last one. "I go back and forth on that. Don't get me wrong, it's not that I don't think AIDS is a big deal, but so much has been written about it, and I want this to be fun, not heavy, you know?" he said. "Sometimes I think that maybe it's impossible to write a fun gay novel. I mean, how can you write about being gay and not write about AIDS? Especially when the characters are as promiscuous as mine are."

"Bar sluts?"

"Isn't everyone?"

I sat there smoking the cigarette. "Is one of the characters based on Mike?"

"Yeah." He looked at the pile of paper. "One of them is based on Mike."

"Is it flattering?"

He looked at me. "I wrote about Mike the way that I saw him."

"And that was how?"

"It wasn't pretty."

I took another cigarette. Great, I was chain-smoking. "I thought you were friends?"

He finished his iced coffee. "Not in the way that you mean."

Interesting. What did I mean? "Well?"

"Mike wasn't capable of being a friend the way most people are friends," he said. "I hate this. You're not supposed to speak ill of the dead."

That's always annoyed me. Someone can go through their life being a major prick. When he drops dead, everyone cries and talks about how they'll miss him. Hypocrisy, thy name is civilization. "Speak ill all you want."

"Mike's priority was Mike." Glen swirled the melting ice around with his straw. "I mean, he cared about me as much as he was capable of. That's not much."

"You loved him?" Glen sounded like what Blaine laughingly called a BSQ: bitter spurned queen.

"Was. I was in love with him. A long time ago. I hadn't been for a long time."

"What happened?"

"He made it clear that I wasn't attractive enough for him." He laughed and rolled his eyes.

I raised my eyebrows. He looked fine to me. "Really?"

He stubbed his cigarette out viciously. "I was too fat for him."

I stared at him in amazement. There was no fat on him anywhere. "You're not fat."

"You should have seen me six months ago." He shook his head. "I weighed 197 pounds, Chanse. I weigh 160 now."

"Congratulations."

"Thanks." He looked down at the table. "I went from a 34 waist to a 29 in six months. It hurt, Chanse. He laughed at me when I asked him out." He looked out the window. There were tears in his eyes. "I mean, I knew I was no great shakes. But I was a nice guy, good sense of humor, and I care about people. Doesn't that count?" He didn't wait for an answer. "Not to Mike. I mean, he went out with that idiot Ronnie Bishop for two years. Two years, Chanse. That guy has the brains of a doorknob. But Ronnie makes $50,000 a year, and Ronnie has a washboard stomach. That's what mattered to Mike."

"I'm sorry."

"Yeah." He sighed and wiped at his eyes. "But I didn't want to talk about Mike."

"Why did you call me?"

"To see if you'd meet me."

Shit. "Um, Glen, I'm kind of seeing someone."

"Of course you are." He started shoving the papers into a bag. "Well, thanks for coming."

"Glen." I grabbed his hand. "I'm not just saying that." Jesus. Why had I dismissed that he might've been attracted to me?

"I know. I'm sorry." He smiled at me again. There were lights behind his eyes. He sighed. "Who was it who said all the good ones are taken?"

"Elizabeth Taylor?"

He laughed at my feeble joke. A good sign. Situation defused. "You want to go for a walk?"

"In this heat?"

"This from a man who drinks hot coffee in the middle of the afternoon in July?"

He finished putting the papers into his bag. I followed him outside. Once outside, he removed his shirt and tucked it into a belt loop. He was wearing very short cutoff Levi's. The fringed denim at the bottom barely covered his butt. He had nice legs, solid and muscular. His muscled torso was completely free of hair, even under his arms. There was a slight pudge to his stomach at the bottom, just below the navel. It was kind of sexy.

We walked in the direction of Jackson Square. The

cracked and tilted sidewalk was crowded with tourists. We weaved in and out of them as they stopped to look into windows. We crossed the street and walked up the steps to the levee. I'd shed my shirt by the time we reached the top. Despite the humidity, the sun felt good on my bare skin. We sat underneath a tree.

"I love the river," Glen said. "I could sit here for hours and watch it."

I looked at the river and saw a lot of muddy water moving by fast.

"There's so much history here," he went on. "Imagine what it must have been like for the French when they came up this huge river with no idea of what lay ahead." He leaned back against the tree. "Tell me about your boyfriend."

"What's to tell?"

"Come on now, don't be shy." He grinned at me again. That smile turned on all the lights in his face. It was beautiful. "You're sort of seeing someone? Why only sort of?"

I pulled a blade of grass out of the ground. "It's been about six weeks."

"Newlyweds? How nice."

"I wouldn't call us newlyweds." What would I call Paul and me? Is there even a name for it? Were we going steady? Dating? "We've just been dating."

"You like him?"

"I guess." That sounded convincing. The truth was I hadn't put a lot of thought into it at all. I had first seen Paul about six weeks earlier at the gym. It was one of my early morning workouts. I was still groggy when I walked in. Paige and I had been to an art opening the night before. Too much wine, too much pot. Alan had given me his chipmunk grin. "New meat in town, Chanse."

"Huh?"

He nodded over in the general direction of the weight area. I turned and saw him. I'm sure Alan claims my jaw hit the floor. On the cable machine, someone was doing standing curls. His biceps were bulging. He had curly dark hair, an incredible tan, and the body! His white ribbed tank top looked about a size too small. It was drenched in sweat, clinging to perfectly shaped muscles. He was wearing a pair of skimpy nylon shorts. The muscles in his legs were strong and lean. His eyes were closed as he fought the pulleys. He finished with an explosive exhalation. The weights slid back down. He opened his eyes. They were a piercing blue. He pulled his tank top up to wipe off his face. The abs looked carved out of marble. There was a trail of curly hair from his navel down to the waistband of his shorts. The navel was pierced. A silver ring stuck out over the line of hair. I had never thought navel piercings were attractive until that moment. I thought I'd never seen anything sexier than the silver ring through his navel.

"Just moved here from Dallas," Alan said.

I turned back to Alan. "So?"

He shrugged. "Thought you might like to know."

I changed. On my way out, I passed him on the way in. He was about 5 foot 11. He smiled at me. His teeth were perfect. "Hey," he said, not stopping.

I couldn't stop thinking about him afterward. Those eyes, the way the tank top had clung to his muscles, the nylon shorts…

I spent that entire day cleaning my apartment. It had been a while since I had cleaned my apartment that thoroughly.

Being horny helped. It'd been a while since I'd gotten laid. I decided to go out that night.

I have a predictable pattern. I start out the evening having a few beers at Cafe Lafitte in Exile. About 11 o'clock I move down Bourbon Street to the Pub. That's where I start looking around at the men. Around 1 o'clock, once I'm feeling a nice buzz, I head over to Oz if there's nobody interesting at the Pub. It was 1:30 when I walked into Oz that night, and I had a good buzz going. I'd also smoked a joint on the balcony at Lafitte's. I walked in. Oz was packed. I got a beer. The dance floor was also crowded. On the stage was the guy from the gym. He was dancing in a pair of tight white jeans shorts with no shirt. His chest glistened with sweat. He tossed his head, shaking damp curls. He was dancing alone. I fought my way through the dance floor. I climbed up on the stage next to him. The music was pumping. I pulled my black T-shirt off, tucked it into a belt loop, and started dancing.

There is something exotic about dancing in a gay bar with your shirt off. I know straight people like to dance. I've been in straight dance clubs. But it never looks like anyone is letting themselves go wild. Dancing in gay bars is seductive. The beat is tribal, incessant. Everyone's stoned out of their gourds. The bass is so loud and strong that it gets into your soul until you can't help but start moving. You give yourself to the music, let it take control of your body. It takes you away. All around you people are dancing with the same abandon. Everyone is into their own mind space. Once in a while the acrid odor of poppers drifts by. Everywhere you look, men are dancing together, covered in sweat, bodies pressed together on the crowded floor. You can't tell who is dancing with who until a butt presses up against a crotch, arms entwine, and the grinding starts. It's fun to dance up on the stage. You can look out over the entire crowd—all gay, all caught up in the moment and the music. There's a sense of community that can't be explained.

The guy from the gym bumped against me.

I looked over at him. He gave me a large smile. "Hey, handsome."

I reached out and touched one of his pecs. It felt as hard as it looked. He took my hand and kissed it. I felt myself getting hard. "Let's get some water," he shouted to me over the music. He jumped off the stage. I followed him to the bar on the second floor. He bought two bottles of water, grabbed my hand and led me out onto the balcony. A bench in the corner was open. We sat down. He put a leg over one of mine.

"My name's Paul." He smiled at me again. "I saw you at the gym today."

"I'm Chanse."

"I know." He took a slug of water. "I asked the guy at the desk what your name was."

Cool, I thought. "Nice to meet you, Paul."

He smiled. "Wanna go back to your place? I'd invite you to mine, but it's a mess. I haven't finished unpacking yet."

I don't have anything against one-night stands. It was the story of my life. I was used to them. They're based on physical attraction, and no one gets hurt, as long as condoms are used. I always find it kind of amusing when I run into a former one-nighter.

Some guys view one-night stands as a possible prelude to a relationship. At least that's what they tell themselves

when they go out looking. I'm not sure why. Is it to justify
fucking a stranger? Or are they really looking for that perfect lover? I haven't been looking for one. Lovers lead to
other things like betrayal and pain, so why bother? Yet
whenever I trick, I play along. I give out my number and
take theirs, knowing that I'd never call. I've had former
one-nighters walk up to me and act pissy. "You never called
me," they always complain. But I'll just say, "Hey, the phone
works both ways": They don't have a comeback to that. We
had fun once, and if you want to have fun again, cool. Don't
act like I owe you something because we got naked.

I weighed the options as Paul sucked on his water bottle.
Hottest guy I've seen in a long time, I thought. *Why the hell not?*
"OK," I said. He gave me a long, wet kiss that brought goose
bumps to my skin.

Paul spent the night. The following morning we went
to the Bluebird for breakfast. After we ate he took me to
his apartment on Carondelet, right off Jefferson close to
Tulane University. He invited me in, and we ended up
stripping each other naked again. I spent the rest of the day
with him, watching his muscles work as he unpacked boxes
naked. It was fun. The following morning he was flying
out on a trip. He promised to call when he got back. He did
call, and our relationship started evolving from there. We
hadn't set boundaries, like not seeing other people. We
were just spending time together and having great sex
when he was in town. What he was doing when he was out
of town, I didn't know. All I knew was that when he was
gone, I didn't venture down to the bars. I had no interest.
Paige thought I was falling in love, but I wasn't so sure. I
was having fun. The sex was great. We got along great. I sort

of missed Paul when he was gone. I wasn't sure what I wanted. I just knew I was enjoying myself spending time with another man for the first time in years. There wasn't anything wrong with that.

Was there? "It started as a one-night stand and kind of went on from there," I said to Glen.

"And they say you won't meet Mr. Right in a bar." Glen shook his head. "Do you love him?"

"I don't know. I'm not thinking in those terms yet."

"Why not?"

I didn't answer him for a while because I couldn't. It had been six weeks, hadn't it? I had no desire to go tricking. I missed him. Was I just lonely? Maybe I was just getting used to having someone around. "I don't know."

He kissed me on the cheek. "You need to think about these things." He stood up. "I've got to get going. I have to work tonight."

"Where do you work?"

"At the airport. I work for Transco. I'm a highly glamorous gate agent." He winked at me. "Window or aisle?"

"I'll walk you home since I'm parked that way." I stood up too. "My boyfriend works for Transco."

"Maybe I know him."

"He's a flight attendant."

"A sky slut, huh?" I must have made a face because he added, "It's a joke, Chanse. We call all of them that. What's his name?"

"Paul Maxwell."

He stopped. "Jesus. You lucky bastard."

"You know him?"

"He's beautiful." Paul started walking again.

We walked to his place in silence. When we reached his gate, he turned to me. "Thanks, Chanse, I enjoyed it. Maybe we could be friends?"

"I'd like that." I meant it. He was a nice guy.

He kissed me on the mouth. I was startled at first. He was nibbling on my lower lip. I started kissing him back.

He pulled away, smiling that damned cute grin of his again. "Call me." Then he was through the door. Gone.

CHAPTER EIGHT

Paige was late as usual. You'd think that by now I'd be used to it. When Paige says 8 o'clock, that's when I should start thinking about getting ready.

But no, at 7 P.M. I was shaving. The clothes I was planning to wear were laid out on my bed. Looking at myself in the mirror, I plucked a few obtrusive nose hairs. Otherwise, not bad, not bad at all. I got into the shower and lathered up. In the background I could hear my stereo. I had three CDs in it on shuffle mode. Stevie Nicks was wailing something about the rooms being on fire.

I like showers like my coffee: hot. Cold showers never make me feel clean. I hate the feeling of the cold spray. The bathroom was filling with steam. I was still a little sore, but it was getting better.

Glen's story was kind of sad. I didn't understand him. How could he stay friends with Mike after being hurt like that? He must have had residual feelings for him. He reminded me of someone else I had known. This person was constantly falling in love with men that treated him like shit. He always made excuses for them. Low self-esteem, I guess.

Dressed, ready to go, and no Paige. It was 8 P.M. already. I swore at myself for getting ready so early. I hate waiting. It drives me crazy. I could have taken a longer nap. I took a long hit off my pipe while I listened to the stereo. It had shuffled Madonna's first CD to the front. Some man was pushing her love over the borderline. I leaned back into the sofa. Big mistake. I started thinking about Glen again.

He was a nice guy. He was attractive. He was intelligent. You've got to have some brains to be writing a book. Of course, it could be a piece of crap. He was a good kisser, though. I remembered the feel of his teeth gently biting into my lower lip. Mike must've been an idiot not to want him. If it weren't for Paul, I'd be all over Glen. But why was that stopping me? What had Paul and I decided? Nothing. We'd never talked about our feelings. We'd never talked about the future. We just took it one day at a time.

Did I want to be involved with someone who was gone at least four days out of the week?

"Sky slut," Glen had said. I'd heard them all: "air mattress," "layover queens," "a boy in every port." What made me think Paul was different? We had never specified monogamy. I just hadn't tricked since that night he picked me up. Was I being foolish in thinking he was the same? I'd slept with flight attendants before—Northwest, American, Delta, US Airways, Southwest, Transco. Plenty of wings in my bed. Some of them had partners wherever they called home. Did I know Paul well enough to trust him? Did I have the right to expect monogamy from him? Were we having an open relationship? Until Paul, it had been one-night stands with tourists who'd be leaving town. I had Paige and Blaine for friendship. I needed to trick once in a while for sexual release. This thing with Paul was rocking my world. I cared about him. He had a great body. He had a decent job.

I was pretty stoned when Paige arrived half an hour late.

Early for her. She breezed in when I opened the door. She went right for the pipe, taking two long, deep hits. "Any booze in the house?" she asked.

I went into the kitchen and poured some Wild Turkey over ice for her.

"Jarrett Phillips is one scary son of a bitch." She took a big gulp of the liquor.

"That why you're late?"

"I'm early." She looked at her watch for confirmation. "I said I'd pick you up at 8. It's 8:37. Usually, I wouldn't be here until 9."

I had to give her that one.

"Besides, they won't break out the top shelf booze at the gallery until at least 9:30. They'll just have one of those cheap boxes of wine. I hate that shit. The good stuff comes out later, you know that."

I gave up on the late issue. I always did. "What gallery?"

"Anderson Galleries." She smiled at me wickedly.

"You bitch." Brian Anderson owned Anderson Galleries. He was a former trick of mine. He was one of those who got mad when I didn't call him after our night together. He didn't call me either. Brian was quite bitchy when he wanted to be. He always wanted to be whenever I was around. This is a classic example of why one should only trick with tourists. With luck, you never have to see them again. Trick with a local, and you run into him all over fucking town.

"I talked to Brian." Paige lit a cigarette. "He's over it already."

"Already? It's been three years," I said. "I should make you go by yourself."

"No way. Then Brian would think you're afraid to face him, that you felt bad, and he'd start telling everyone that. Can't you just hear him?" She rolled her eyes and mimicked his drawl perfectly. "Big, strong, old Chanse MacLeod is afraid to face me because of the way he treated me about a one-night stand. Can you imagine?" She laughed.

I sighed. "You're right." She could win an argument with Satan. I hate that about her sometimes.

"What did you do today?"

I filled her in on my conversation with Glen. I omitted the fact that Glen kissed me. That information was on a need-to-know basis. Paige didn't need to know. She liked Paul a lot. She wanted us to make it to happily ever after.

"I thought you weren't interested in this." Paige blew smoke in the general direction of the ceiling. "Mike sounds like he was a real prize."

"It keeps popping up in my life." I stood. "Shall we go?"

"I'll drive," Paige said. I suppressed a wince. I'd kissed the ground when I got out of the car the first time I had ridden with her. Traffic laws meant nothing to Paige. Her driving theory was "drive offensively." Everyone else drove defensively, right? This way everyone would get out of her way. Frightening as her driving was, she had never been in an accident or gotten a ticket. She often let her tags and registration expire. Her insurance was constantly being canceled because she forgot to pay it. Riding with Paige was always an adventure.

We made it to the Quarter with only two near-death experiences. Paige found a spot to park on Dumaine between Chartres and Royal. She has a sixth sense about parking spots. She can always find one immediately. There was a nice cool breeze blowing down from the river. She looked pretty in her black miniskirt and her red blouse. The gallery was on Royal just past Toulouse. The gallery was ablaze with light. It was full of people dressed to the teeth. I didn't understand it. The temperature still had to be in the 90s. My legs were sweating in the loose-fitting khakis I was wearing. How could people be wearing blazers?

The minute we walked in, Brian Anderson descended upon us. "Paige! Chanse! So glad you could make it!" Brian was about 5 foot 10 and pale, with receding curly reddish-blond hair. His face was covered with freckles. He worked out regularly at the New Orleans Athletic Club. His body showed it. His eyes were pale blue and round. He looked like someone had choked him just long enough to make his eyes bug out a bit. He was semiattractive.

I wondered whatever possessed me to pick him up that night at Lafitte's. He'd been wearing a pair of black leather minishorts, a chain-link harness, and a black leather baseball cap. I generally don't go for the leather look. But I'd had a few shots of Wild Turkey, and he has a nice body. When I was drunk, he seemed funny and charming. Hung over the next morning, he was annoying. He talked with his jaw stuck out. He drew out his words. I guess the idea was to sound cultured and private-schooled. It came across as pompous.

He kissed us both on the cheek. His eyes peered into mine and then he turned back to Paige. "Darling, you look fabulous!"

"Thanks."

"Paige, I think you'll like our artist." He took her by the arm, ignoring me. Well, that was better than being bitchy.

I made my way over to the refreshment table. I got a glass of red wine from a tuxedoed bartender who looked familiar. He winked, and I winked back. I guess the tight shirt looked good on me. Cool. I wandered over to a wall and stared at one of the paintings. It looked like someone had fired paint pellets at a piece of canvas. I don't understand art.

"Crap, isn't it?" A voice said behind me. I turned and saw a tall, handsome man wearing dress jeans and a red knit pullover. "We can thank Picasso for this shit."

He didn't introduce himself. Fine. "I don't know much about art."

"You know enough to see this is shit," he sniffed. He was holding a glass of red wine. He was a little shorter than me. His skin was olive, with thick bluish black hair. His teeth were big and white. "I can't believe Brian is trying to pass this off as art."

"Abel!" Brian and Paige joined us. His face looked red. "You don't like the textures she used in this piece?" Brian grabbed his arm and led him away.

"Who was that?" I whispered to Paige.

"You amaze me." She giggled. She'd had a few glasses of wine. "You don't know who anyone is, do you?"

"No."

"That's Abel Fontenot."

The name was vaguely familiar. "That should mean something to me?"

"He's Jarrett's right-hand man over at Gay Rights Now!" Paige said. "He's the development director."

I raised my eyebrows.

"That means he raises all of their money for them," Paige said.

Brian walked back up, mopping his forehead with a napkin.

"Are you OK?" Paige slipped an arm through his.

"Abel can be such a prick." Brian shook his head. "I mean, the artist donated all of these paintings for this damned fund-raiser, and now he's afraid the work isn't good enough and might make GRN look bad." He rolled his eyes. "Like he knows art!"

"This is a fund-raiser?" I asked.

"Whatever is sold here tonight, GRN gets the money." Brian replied. "Paige tells me you found Mike Hansen's body the other day," Brian went on. "Did you hear about what happened at Lafitte's on Sunday night?"

"No."

"Well, you know I don't tell tales out of school," Brian smiled, teeth gleaming. "But I was at Lafitte's when Justin Warren came storming in. He was in quite a mood, I can tell you. He was looking for Remy. I had just seen Remy at Domino's with Mike Hansen. Really, if you're going to cheat on your lover you should be much more discreet. Like people don't talk!"

"What did you tell Justin?" I asked.

"I didn't tell him I'd just seen his partner with the town tramp at Domino's," Brian said, rolling his eyes. "That's not my style. I just said I hadn't seen him. Far be it from me to rain on anyone's parade. Poor old Remy. It must get dreadful to get old and have men only interested in your money." He stroked his chin thoughtfully. "Though I suppose the person I should truly feel sorry for would be Justin."

"Why's that?"

"Is there anything sadder than a boy toy who's gotten too old but is used to the money?" Brian shook his head. "I mean, what could Justin do? He's just a nurse, after all. That kind of salary isn't going to get him a house on Esplanade, is it?"

"Well, he'd hardly have to go to a mission," Paige said.

"Macaroni and cheese tastes much worse when you're used to caviar, darling."

He was starting to get on my nerves. I like macaroni and cheese. "What happened then?"

"Justin got an Absolut tonic and told me that he didn't know what to do," Brian said. "Apparently, Remy had been running around with Mike Hansen. Justin was simply heartsick about the entire thing. He said he'd like to kill that hard-bodied little bitch."

"He said that?" Paige interjected.

Brian nodded. "Exact words, darling. 'I'd like to kill that hard-bodied little bitch.'"

I took a deep breath. "Did you talk to the police?"

"The police?" Brian did a double take. "What on earth for?"

"You heard someone threaten to kill someone who was killed the very next day, you boob."

"Of course I didn't tell the police!" He set his jaw. "Justin spoke to me in confidence. I couldn't betray his trust."

"Come on, Chanse, let's go," Paige pulled me out onto Royal Street. She pulled a cigarette out of her purse and lit it.

"What did you do that for?"

"You were about to cause a scene." She puffed on her cigarette. "Yes, Brian should go to the police. You and I know that. But Brian doesn't think like a normal person."

"Stupid queen." I started walking back to the car.

"You can call Venus in the morning and tell her." Paige flicked her cigarette into the gutter. "I'm sure this is a more promising lead than any of the bullshit Jarrett Phillips is handing her."

"What exactly did Jarrett Phillips tell you today anyway?"

"The same old conspiracy bullshit," Paige said. "The police and straight people in general wish all the gays were dead, there's a group of right-wing religious fanatics that wants to kill all the gays in New Orleans, and it's starting now." She shrugged. "Maybe he's right."

FAGGOTS DIE.

I saw the wall again in my head.

"Are you OK?"

"Fine. I shivered just a little. You know, Jarrett showed up at Mike's apartment yesterday."

An eyebrow went up. "What was he doing there?"

"He said that he had an appointment with Mike." I shrugged. "I didn't think much about it."

We had reached the car. "Mike did some volunteer work at a fund-raiser for Jarrett's group. Basically, he was a go-go boy at a party in Uptown about a month ago. All he did was dance on a speaker in a G-string. But that's enough for Jarrett to think that someone killed Mike as a warning to him to stop his work for gay rights. And he thinks this is just the beginning."

I got into the car. "Oh, please. Does he really think there's a group of fanatics out there ready to kill gays? And why on earth would they start by killing a go-go boy from one of his fund-raisers?"

FAGGOTS DIE.

MURDER IN THE RUE DAUPHINE

Paige smiled at me wickedly. "Oh, Mike was more than just a go-go boy to Jarrett."

"Huh?"

"Mike and Jarrett had been dating."

I picked my jaw up off the floorboards. "Mike and Jarrett?"

"Mike was a busy little boy." Paige started the car and pulled out of her spot without checking to see if anything was coming. There was a screech of tires and some honking. She ignored it and headed up Dumaine. "He was seeing Jarrett Phillips, and it seems like he was involved with Remy Deveraux and…"

"And?"

"There was someone else too. Jarrett knew that Mike was seeing someone else, but it wasn't Remy Deveraux he was talking about."

"How do you know it wasn't Remy?"

"Jarrett didn't know the guy's name. All he knew was the guy had a lot of money. Everybody in town seems to have known about Remy."

"Someone with a lot of money," I mused, looking out the window at a bunch of tourists weaving on the sidewalk. One of the girls leaned against the wall. I looked away, but not fast enough to avoid seeing the stream of vomit. Ah, tourists.

"Exactly. Any ideas?"

"Had to be the guy who was being blackmailed."

"Where did he find the time for all of these men?" Paige ran a yellow light at Canal that turned red before we crossed the street. More honking.

"And more importantly, did any of these men know about the other ones?"

"Jarrett didn't know about Remy. I'm pretty sure he would have told me if he'd known."

We rode in silence for a while. Well, silent except for horns blaring and the sound of tires abruptly screeching to a stop on pavement as Paige cut people off and ran stop signs. She dropped me off at my front door. Her eyes glittered dangerously in the glow of the streetlights. "Oh, by the way, when were you planning on telling me that it might have been a hate crime?" She put the car in gear, then roared off.

I let myself into the house. How the hell had Paige found that out? Maybe Venus changed her mind about releasing the information. Not my problem. I walked over to the answering machine. I picked up my pipe and took another hit. There was one message. I hit the play button.

Beep. "Chanse, this is Glen. I just wanted to call you and let you know that I really enjoyed myself this afternoon. I also want to apologize for kissing you. You're seeing someone, and it was totally wrong of me to do that. I hope we can still be friends."

The machine clicked off. No message from Paul? I started undressing. I found a pack of cigarettes in my underwear drawer and lit one. Surely he hadn't had another late flight.

Sky slut, flying mattress, sky slut…

I got under the covers. In the morning I'd call Venus and tell her what I had found out. Then I would be out of this thing.

After all, I don't do murders.

CHAPTER NINE

I woke up in a bad mood.

The sun was shining through the curtains. According to my alarm clock it was 9:30. I hadn't set it. I'd planned on sleeping until I woke up. Not waking up to an alarm is one of the great pleasures of my life. I sat on the couch in my underwear with a cup of coffee and switched on the television. I watched a rerun of *The Love Boat* while the coffee woke me up. I wondered what Charo was up to these days.

I started getting dressed for the gym. It wasn't going to be a good workout, though, so I decided not to go. Every muscle still ached. I was entitled to a day off.

That decision made, I called Venus.

"Casanova." She answered on the first ring.

"Venus, it's Chanse." For a minute I wondered if she might be territorial about her investigation. What the hell. If she got pissed, she got pissed. I told her what I had learned from Alan, Glen, and Brian.

"I'll check it out," she said. Click.

"Bitch," I said to the phone. I walked into the bathroom and stared in the mirror. "You don't do murders," I said to my reflection. I took a long hot shower. My skin was reddish when I got out. I got dressed and walked out the front door to catch the St. Charles streetcar.

Remy Deveraux's office was at Place St. Charles. In a past

life, I think Place St. Charles was a department store. Now it's a collection of extremely expensive small shops and boutiques for the business people of downtown. There were several floors of offices above Place St. Charles. I walked in out of the heat and avoided a group of women in business attire. They were too busy talking to notice me. They were carrying to-go cups of iced coffee. Not even an "excuse me" as they passed. What ever happened to manners? I headed for the elevators. It was 11:30. Maybe Remy was in his office.

Remy's office was on the 23rd floor. I looked around when I got off the elevator. Office space in Place St. Charles was expensive, but Remy was doing pretty well. He had redone a mansion in the Garden District for our local supernatural best-selling author. It had earned him the cover of *Architectural Digest.* When my landlady had gotten bored with her Garden District mansion, she'd hired him to do it over. It was a good job. I'd seen it when she invited me to her "redecoration party." It was a little ornate for my taste.

I pushed through the glass doors of his office and approached the receptionist. "I'd like to see Remy," I told her with what I hoped was a disarming smile.

"Do you have an appointment?" she asked. Her hair was obviously dyed black and shellacked into a helmet. She was wearing too much makeup. *The dragon guarding the gates,* I thought.

"If I'd had one I would've said so."

"Mr. Deveraux is extremely busy." She tapped the top of her desk with sharp red nails.

"Why don't you ask him if he'll see me?"

She rolled her eyes. "Name?"

"Chanse MacLeod." I was tempted to add that I had a $4 million renovation project that I was planning on hiring him for. Did she treat his clients in this rude, bored manner? "Tell him I want to talk to him about Mike Hansen."

Her facial expression clearly said "whatever" but she picked up the phone and called back. "Mr. Deveraux, there's a Chanse MacLeod here to see you about Mike Hansen." She said the words like I were something she'd stepped in. "All right." She hung up the phone. "He'll be right out." She didn't look surprised. She also didn't drop the attitude.

Remy Deveraux stepped through the door behind her. He was wearing a white linen suit. His hair was thinning. I was reasonably certain that its yellowish-blond shade wasn't natural. He was tanned with that orangish tint that belied actual sun. He sported more than his share of wrinkles. He was maybe 5 foot 10. He stuck out his hand. "Good to see you again, Chanse." I shook his hand. His palms were moist. "Have you had lunch yet?"

"No."

"Why don't you join me?"

"OK."

We got into the elevators. "Is your receptionist always so charming?" I asked.

He sighed. "Bernice has been with me since I opened my office. She's had it rough."

Who hasn't? I thought as we walked out onto St. Charles. We walked up Poydras to Le Pavilion. Le Pavilion was one of the historic hotels of the city. He kept pulling a handkerchief to mop the sweat off his face. We were escorted to a table.

"The salad bar here is magnificent," Remy said once we'd ordered our drinks. I got iced tea. He got white wine.

"Sounds good to me." We walked into the main dining room. He was right. I'd never seen a salad bar quite like this. They had everything. I helped myself to a heaping plate and went back to the table.

"So what do you want to know about Mike Hansen?" he asked after he rejoined me.

"Remy, I know something was going on between you two." I dabbed at my face with a napkin. "I don't know you or Justin well, but I know you've been together a long time. What gives?"

"Are you investigating his death?"

"Unofficially," I said. "I know that Justin threatened to kill Mike on Sunday night, and then Monday afternoon Mike turned up dead. Doesn't look good for Justin."

He sighed. "He couldn't kill anyone, Chanse. It was one of those heat-of-the-moment things, you know?" He went on when I didn't respond. "We've been together for 14 years. He was a kid when we started, only 20. A couple of years ago, he became sexually curious."

"What?"

"I was the only man he'd ever been with." Remy took a big gulp of wine. "It was kind of like a marital crisis. He wasn't sure of himself or how he felt anymore. Our relationship had gotten stale and boring for him, I guess is the best way to put it. He wanted some time apart so he could figure out what he wanted."

"And?"

"Well, I didn't want to do that." Remy rubbed his forehead. "I'm not a young man, Chanse. Oh, I pretend that

I'm not old, but the mirror doesn't lie to me. I love Justin. What if he went out and found something better? Someone younger? What then? So, I made a deal with him. We would try to expand our sexual horizons."

"And how did you do that?"

"We started having three-ways." Remy finished off the wine and signaled for more. Once his glass was refilled, he went on. "At first, I'd just call up and order an escort. Then we started cruising the bars for thirds. The arrangement was that neither one of us would have a sexual outing without the other. It worked. It made Justin happy, it revitalized our sex life, everything was fine. And then came Mike Hansen." His face darkened. "We picked him up one night at Oz. At the time, I thought the reason he came with us was for free coke, you know? But it was fun, and we enjoyed ourselves. Mike gave us his number and told us to call him anytime. Well, Justin invited him over for dinner the next week."

"How many times did you guys sleep with him?"

"Four or five." Remy looked at his lap. "Then Mike decided that he didn't want to have three-ways anymore. At least, not if Justin was involved. I was shocked, flattered. I mean, did you ever meet Mike Hansen? The looks of a porn star and hung like a horse. It's hard to explain, but at my age you get used to being considered old by all the pretty young boys."

"Jesus."

"He said that Justin didn't interest him, emotionally or sexually. But I did. He said that I was sexy and mature." Remy stabbed a cucumber with his fork. "I didn't believe him at first. He kept calling, wanting to get together, just the two of us. He called me at home; he called me at the office. Finally, I agreed to see him. I told Justin I was seeing him to get him to leave me alone."

"And?"

"I slept with him."

I looked at him. The dyed hair. The tanned skin. *Is this what life has in store for me as I get older?* I wondered. *The eternal attempt to stay young forever?* "How many times?"

"It was a big mistake." Remy mopped his forehead again. "Justin was hurt. I promised I wouldn't do it again. But when Mike called me a few days later, I went. He was a sexy guy, Chanse, but I didn't love him. It sounds pathetic, but it was nice to feel sexy and young and attractive. The whole thing with Justin exploring his sexuality, well, it made me feel like I was losing it. Mike made me feel like I was everything that I'd been."

"That must've thrilled Justin."

"I love Justin, Chanse." He pierced a tomato with his fork. "I never planned on leaving him, or throwing him out and having Mike take his place." He laughed bitterly. "Sometimes I think that was Justin's major concern. Not that I was going to fall in love with someone else, but that I was going to throw him out."

Ouch. "He said that?"

"Not in so many words." He began pushing pieces of lettuce around with his fork. "I'm not stupid, Chanse. I know I'm getting older. I know Justin is younger than me. I know he could go out and find someone else. It would be harder for me. I know part of the reason Justin stays with me is because of the money."

"You don't think Justin loves you?"

"Justin loves the life I've given him. He loves me too. I don't know which he loves better."

"Then what happened?"

"I decided it was over with Mike and me. I made a date with him for dinner on Sunday night. We went to Domino's and then to Good Friends for a drink. At the bar I told him I wasn't going to see him anymore."

"How did he react?"

Remy's face clouded. "He just laughed and said that was fine with him. He had found someone else, you see, someone younger with more money."

"Oh."

He nodded. "I was about to leave when Justin got there. He was furious. He slapped Mike and called him all sorts of names. The bouncer had to come over and ask us to leave."

"Remy, I'm sorry."

"It was a shock." He laughed and pushed his plate away. "I felt like an old fool. All the suspicions I'd been having about Justin and my money—while all the time I thought Mike cared. It was the money he wanted. He was no different than what I thought Justin had turned into." He sighed. "Maybe what Justin's always been."

"How did you feel about Mike after Sunday night?"

"Betrayed. Hurt. A little angry." He shrugged. An amused grin spread over his face. "Are you asking me if I killed him?"

"Did you?"

"No. I was in my office in a meeting with a client all day Monday." Remy lit a cigarette. "When I heard what happened, I was glad I had an alibi. I'm surprised that the police haven't come around asking questions."

"What about Justin?"

"What about him?"

"He certainly had a reason for killing Mike, didn't he?" I was kind of surprised this hadn't occurred to him. "He was afraid of losing you to Mike. You said yourself that Justin didn't want to give up the life you've provided for him all of these years. Why not Justin?"

"He couldn't kill anyone." Remy dismissed this notion with a flick of ash into the ashtray. "I've lived with him for almost 15 years. I'd know."

Famous last words. "You aren't sure if he loves you, but you know him enough to say he couldn't kill anyone?"

"There was no motive anyway." Remy's eyes hardened. "He knew it was over between Mike and me on Sunday night. I told him."

"You'd never told him that before?"

Remy's jaw dropped. "Well, yes, but—"

"So why should he believe you this time?"

"I…"

"Well," I wiped my mouth with my napkin, "I think it's something you should think about." I had gotten more than I'd bargained for. "I think you should probably give Venus Casanova at the police a call."

"The police? Why?"

"If I found out that Justin threatened to kill Mike in front of witnesses, Venus will. It'd look better if you went to her first. Hell, she might not even be interested." She didn't seem to be when I talked to her. There was no reason for him to know that she already knew.

Remy paid for lunch with a credit card. "Chanse, I would appreciate it if you didn't tell anyone about this."

"No one to tell."

"Thanks." We walked back to Place St. Charles together. I'm sure Remy was sorry he'd told me so much. He'd needed someone outside of his social circle to talk to. I'd filled in nicely. But things were going to be awkward for him now whenever he saw me. It didn't happen often, but it did happen. I said goodbye to him as he disappeared into the building.

I started walking in the direction of the Quarter. I didn't think Remy killed Mike. He was a possibility, though. Maybe he'd been trying out his story on me. It was hot. I was sweating. I took my shirt off. When I reached St. Ann, I walked up to Good Friends.

Good Friends Bar was almost completely deserted when I walked in. A couple of the neighborhood lushes were having their early afternoon cocktails. The bartender on duty was Rafe Thibodeaux. I knew Rafe slightly. He was a nice-looking guy, black hair, brown eyes almost black, with a slight paunch to his stomach. His teeth were crooked. "Hey, Chanse. Draft?"

"Nah, give me a Coke." He placed it in front of me. I gave him a five, waving off the change.

"What's up?"

"Were you on duty yesterday?"

"Yep." He began wiping the bar.

"Were you here when Justin Warren came in?"

"You mean when he caught Remy with Mike?" he grinned. "Yeah. Right in front of me, in fact. It got ugly for a minute, there. Had to get the bouncer. Justin just wanted to let out some steam, I guess. Then him and Remy left."

"What did Mike do then?"

"He finished his drink and left."

"Do you know where he went?"

"Pub, probably." Rafe cocked his head at me. "Shame about him getting killed."

"Did you know him well?"

"As well as I know anyone who comes in here," he said. "About as well as I know you."

"Thanks, Rafe." I finished my Coke.

The bartenders at the Pub weren't much help. Yes, Mike had been in on Sunday night. No, they didn't know if he'd left alone.

I walked back out onto the street. Time to go talk to Justin.

CHAPTER TEN

I headed down Bourbon Street toward Esplanade. I was kind of in shock. I knew gay relationships operated under different rules. Blaine and his partner had an open relationship. They'd been together over 10 years. Remy and Justin seemed to have sort of an agreement to let a third person into their bed whenever they chose. I thought about other long term couples that I knew. What were their arrangements?

So much for monogamy.

Someone called my name as I crossed Dumaine, and I turned. "Hey!"

It was Glen Chandler. He walked up to me with that big smile on his face. He was wearing a pair of black Lycra bicycle pants and a red tank top. He had his bag slung over his shoulder. He gave me a quick hug. "What brings you to the Quarter again?"

"Just checking up on some things." I smiled. He shook out a cigarette. He offered me one. I lit and savored it.

"I don't think you're ready to quit smoking yet." He shook his head. We stepped into the shade offered by Lafitte's Guest House. "Did you get my message?"

"Yeah. That was nice of you." I felt embarrassed. I hadn't called back. "I got in late last night and have been on the go since I woke up." I was babbling. "I would've called you."

"It's OK." He dismissed the entire thing with a wave of his cigarette. "You have a boyfriend, right? We're just friends." He took a deep drag off his cigarette. "What are you checking up on?"

"Mike still."

"Aren't the police handling it?"

"Yeah." I sat on the stoop. "It just seems to keep popping up in my life."

"Drag," Glen commiserated.

"Did you know Mike was involved with Justin Warren and Remy Deveraux?"

"Who didn't?" Glen grinned at me. "I couldn't figure that one out. Just between you and me, I was fucked up one night, and they nabbed me at the Parade. Not a fun night at all." He shuddered. "Didn't make any sense to me. Mike was particular. Not his usual type at all. I figured it was the money." He made a face.

"Did you know that he was also seeing Jarrett Phillips?"

"I wouldn't call it seeing." Glen sat on the stoop beside me. "He let Jarrett take him to dinner a couple of times. Mike didn't sleep with him. Jarrett didn't want to sleep with him either. Mike said he was into some weird shit, though."

"Like what?"

"Never said." Glen stubbed his cigarette out. "Who knows? People get their kicks all kinds of ways. I could tell you stories," he said. "It's tough to be single."

"Yeah."

"Right." He winked at me. "You're lucky. You're sort of seeing someone. Hey, look, I'm going to Kaldi's to work on my book for a while. Wanna join me?"

"Gonna be there for a while?"

"A few hours, at least."

"I'll meet you there." He gave me a quick goodbye kiss on the cheek. I watched him go. He had a round, small, solid ass. Very nice.

I walked down to Esplanade and turned left. The Deveraux-Warren manse was between Burgundy and Rampart. I put my shirt on when I reached the wrought iron gate. It was a Victorian, painted a pale yellow with gray trim. I walked through the gate. Two recumbent stone lions guarded the steps to the porch. On my way up I patted one on the head. I rang the doorbell.

"Yes?" Justin Warren was about 6 foot 1. He was wearing a white nurse's uniform. He had pale white skin. His hair and eyes were a deep black. The bags under his eyes made him look older than he was. He was slender and long-boned.

"Hey, Justin. Don't you remember me?" I stuck my hand out. "Chanse MacLeod. We met at Barbara Castlemaine's renovation party."

"Oh, yes, the private eye," he said tiredly. "Remy called and said you might be coming by." He turned and walked into the shadows inside. "Come in."

Despite all the windows the house was completely dark. He led me through several darkened rooms. He pushed open a door. I was momentarily blinded. The kitchen was all windows and sunlight. "Can I offer you something to drink?"

"Some tea if you have it."

He got a pitcher of tea from the refrigerator. He filled two glasses with ice, added tea to one, and handed it to me.

A lemon wedge was floating in it. He reached into cabinet and withdrew a gallon jug of gin. He filled his glass, then sat down on a barstool. "All right, I've played hostess. What do you want?"

"Just to talk about a few things."

"Like Mike Hansen?" Justin smiled with one side of his mouth. "You think I killed him?"

"Don't know. Did you?"

"No." He took a gulp from the glass. "Should've, though. Would've made everyone's lives a lot easier."

"Interesting thought."

He started laughing. "Yeah, gonna run to that big bull dyke cop and tattle on me?"

Weird how everyone thought Venus was a lesbian. "Why don't you tell me how it all happened?"

He put the glass down. "Look at me." I did. "What do you see? Some tired old housewife with a career to keep him busy? I make less than a tenth of what Remy does. He has Family Money too." Those words are always capitalized in New Orleans. "I met him when I was 20. Living on macaroni and cheese and Ramen. Busting my ass working 30 hours a week and putting myself through nursing school. Remy changed all of that." He looked away. "He took me out of my shithole apartment. I quit my job and just studied. I got this beautiful house in the Quarter. I drive a BMW. If I don't want to work, I don't have to." He refilled the glass. "There was only one other man before Remy. I'm getting old. I wanted some fun."

"Yeah, Remy told me."

"And he was a saint about it. Went along with it. Anything I wanted. And things were fine. Then Mike came along."

He took a drink out of the glass. "Did you meet him? When he was alive?"

I nodded.

"Looked like a porn star. And a nice guy? He could charm the pants right off of you. I couldn't believe it when he approached me at Oz."

"He approached you?"

"Is that so hard to believe?"

Frankly, yes. He wasn't the type of guy I would picture Mike with. There wasn't anything wrong with him, but he wasn't the kind of guy that caught your eye from across the room. "No."

"Thanks for the lie," he said. "I couldn't believe it either. The sex was incredible—every fantasy I ever had come to life. He would try anything. And he kept coming back. Then he wanted just Remy. I should've seen it coming."

"He tried to break you up?"

"Little hard-bodied gold-digging slut. That's what he was." He spat the words out. "How do you think I felt when Mike said that he didn't want me anymore? That he just wanted Remy? Remy was flattered. I knew what the little whore was after." He waved his hands. "He was after this. He wanted my life, the whore. And Remy! How could he be such an old fool to think someone like that would be attracted to him? How could anyone be that incredibly blind?"

"People are attracted to all different types."

"Not that little whore." He refilled his glass with gin. "You think I hadn't seen him around before? Noticed him in the bars? Always with some guy with a hot body. And then he wants to come home with me and Remy. And me, blinded by his muscles and big dick, I thought he wanted me and was willing to put up with Remy." He slammed his drink down, splashing liquid on the butcher block. "Well, I wasn't going to stand for it."

"What were you going to do?"

He gave me a sickly smile. "My name is on the deed to this house. All of our accounts have both names on them. Mike wasn't going to be getting nearly as much money as he thought he was."

"So you were going to make the breakup financially difficult?"

"Remy also signed a contract five years ago, promising to take care of me for the rest of my life." He picked the drink back up and finished it. "I was getting a lawyer."

"I hear you hit Mike on Sunday night."

"Bartenders sure love to talk, don't they? No more tips for Rafe." He put the glass in the sink. "Yeah, I was pissed. Remy had lied to me again. He tells me he's going to go for a walk and to check out some furniture that just came in at one of the shops on Royal, and that he might stop in for a drink at Lafitte's on his way back." He rolled his eyes. "I'm always amazed at how stupid Remy sometimes thinks I am. I knew he was meeting the little whore. I just didn't know where. So I waited an hour or two and went down to Lafitte's. I was going to say that I decided to join him for a drink. I ran into that bitchy Brian Anderson there—didn't you sleep with him once?"

This town lives and revolves around gossip, I swear. "Maybe."

"Don't like to admit it?" He gave me that cold smile again. "Little Miss Bitch Brian was only too happy to tell me that he'd seen Remy and Mike together at Domino's." So much for Brian not raining on anyone's parade. "And he thought they were going to Good Friends. So I walked down there, not wanting to believe him. Sure enough, there they were, talking and laughing without a care in the world." He picked up the bottle of gin and put it away. "I put a stop to that right then and there. I walked in, slapped the whore right across the face, and dragged Remy's ass back home with me where it belongs. End of story."

"Didn't you tell Brian that you wanted to kill Mike?"

He shrugged. "Maybe. I'd had a few drinks. I don't remember much of what I told him."

"Did you know that Mike was seeing a man with money? A closeted doctor from Uptown?"

"Remy mentioned something about it to me. I hadn't talked to Mike since I realized he was trying to steal my life."

"No idea who it was?"

"Nope."

"So where were you during the afternoon the day before yesterday?"

"Here. By myself. I took the day off from the hospital."

"Anyone see you?"

"No." He leered at me. "I don't have an alibi. But I didn't shoot the whore. If I'd killed him, it would've been a much more painful death than a gunshot. I guarantee you that."

"Thanks. I'll see myself out." I left him drinking in the kitchen.

I wanted to take a hot shower. Talking to him made me feel like I'd been dipped in slime. I stood there, letting the sun reheat my cold limbs. So far I'd learned that Mike had dumped Justin, that Remy may or may not have dumped

Mike (or vice versa), that Justin hated Mike enough to kill him, and that Jarrett and Mike were into something kinky. Maybe Mike's murder was a kinky game gone wrong? It was an option, at least.

I started walking toward the river. Poor Remy. All the gossip had been right. Justin was in it for the money. And he could use this little affair of Remy's with Mike to his own advantage. In fact, I was sure that Justin was doing everything he could to suck Remy in deeper. I wouldn't be surprised if Justin came out of this entire thing with full title to the house. He wouldn't risk all that financial gain by committing a crime. And he seemed too cold to care enough to kill Mike.

I wondered if prostituting yourself left you empty and dead inside.

When I was at LSU, I had a chance. One of the alumni, old Mississippi money, saw me at a banquet. He invited me to his mansion for dinner. He took me for a stroll on the grounds after we ate. He was in his late 70s. He offered to put me up in a town house in New Orleans with a $4,000-a-month allowance. All I had to do was be available to him one weekend out of the month. I politely turned him down. Later, during rough times when I wondered where the rent was going to come from, I'd remember that and wonder what my life would've been like if I'd said yes.

Now I know.

CHAPTER ELEVEN

My mind reeled as I walked to Kaldi's.

What kind of person was Mike Hansen? I'm a good judge of character, but he'd fooled me. I'd thought he was a nice guy with a problem. He wasn't a nice guy. He'd been willing to sell his body to the highest bidder. I have problems with that. Maybe I shouldn't be so judgmental, but it was just something I couldn't do myself. I don't like the idea of going to bed with someone that I'm not attracted to. Yeah, I've been a bar tramp like everyone else. I've gone to bed with guys whose last names I never knew. Money never changed hands, though. I could never live the life Mike was trying to make for himself. I hadn't met anyone who had anything nice to say about him. How sad to die with no one able to say anything nice about you. Nobody was mourning him. No one was sorry he was dead. The people who'd known him were ready to pin a medal on the killer's chest.

Besides, I don't do murders.

I walked into Kaldi's. The place was packed with kids. Maybe they weren't kids. Maybe I was just getting old. Tattoos, piercings, and clothes that were little more than rags abounded. Why are kids determined to make themselves so ugly? Glen waved at me from over by a window. I got myself a cup of coffee. The jukebox was blaring an old Billie Holiday song.

I sat at Glen's table. "Hey."

"What's wrong?" He lit a cigarette, closing his notebook.

"Nothing," I said. "Everything."

"I'm sorry." He squeezed my hand.

I took a sip of my coffee. "Glen, you knew Mike better than anyone, right?"

"I guess. I don't know. Sometimes I think I didn't know him at all."

"What kind of person was he?"

"Do I look like a shrink?" He half smiled at me. He took a deep breath. "I don't know, Chanse. I used to wonder if he wasn't so goddamned gorgeous if I would've bothered with him. You know, being friends. He could be mean when he wanted to, but it always seemed like he didn't know he was being mean, you know? He used to say the cruelest things to me, and then be shocked when I got mad or upset, like I was crazy or something. He could be sweet too. One night we were at Oz. This guy started coming on to me. He was cute, so I flirted back with him. We kissed a few times, and then he just got crazy on me. He grabbed my arm and started calling me names, and he hurt me. I thought he'd sprained my wrist or something, and then Mike was right there and tore the guy off of me and knocked him down. He walked me home, put me to bed, and stayed there with me the whole night, just to make sure I was OK." He laughed bitterly. "Later I thought maybe he was pissed because he was the only person allowed to fuck with me."

"Did Mike ever hurt you physically?"

"No." He took a long drag off the cigarette. "When I was 20, I got involved with this guy who was literally nuts. At the time, I used to think—oh, I hate to say this, but what the hell, right?" He gave me a smile that was most definitely cynical. "I grew up in a very Christian family. I was taught from the cradle that people like me were going straight to hell. I was a freak, a pervert, and could never be happy, unless I married some girl and had a family and stayed in the church. I fell in love with a guy who was straight, or so he said. It was hell. We had sex together, but he made me feel like I was corrupting him. He really liked women, you see. He was abusive, physically and mentally. I left him when he broke my arm." He stubbed out his cigarette, lit another. "I told Mike that, and he was sweet about it. He was always ready to jump to my defense if someone looked like they were going to hit me or something. It was nice, and I loved him for it. But he was cruel sometimes." He blinked back tears. "I never knew what to think. I used to think that I was perfect for him, that I'd make him happy the way no one else could. But I don't think Mike wanted to be happy."

"Does anyone?"

"That's cynical." He flicked ash out the window. "I want to be happy. I want to find that one special person to spend the rest of my life with, have the white picket fence and the English setters and the whole ball of wax. I mean, I might be getting old, but I'm holding out for love." He smiled at me. "What about you?"

"Me?"

"Yes, you."

"I guess it would be nice to fall in love."

"You're not in love with Paul?"

"No." As soon as I said it, I knew it was true. I wasn't in love with Paul. I liked him a lot; I enjoyed being with him. The sex was great, but I wasn't in love with him. "At least not yet."

"Well, I wish you the best." He smiled at me, but it wasn't the big smile. It was sad.

"I don't even know if it's possible for me to fall in love." What was I saying?

"You don't?" His eyes opened wide. "Why not? My God, Chanse, that's the whole point of life. Love. Falling in love. Finding that special person you want to spend your life with."

"You've watched too many Disney movies."

"And what if I have?" Glen asked, his voice quiet. "Is it wrong to want to find someone special? Someone that will love me?"

"Maybe."

"What do you want, Chanse?"

"I don't know." I'd gone down that road once. It was the biggest mistake of my life. There's no such thing as romantic love. It's just a gimmick, something to sell cards and candy and flowers. It's a conspiracy force-fed down our throats from the time we are children. All we have to look forward to when we grow up are shattered dreams and broken hearts. I looked across the table at Glen. I couldn't tell him that. He still bought into it. I wasn't going to tell him there's no Santa Claus.

"You're going to fall hard for someone one day," he said, grinning at me. Full wattage this time.

"Nah." I grinned back at him. "Say, did Mike ever tell you about this rich doctor he was seeing?"

"Rich doctor?" Glen looked at me like I'd lost my mind. "What are you talking about?"

"That's why Mike hired me," I said. "Someone was black-mailing his boyfriend. He was in the closet, and being outed at this point in his life would have caused some heavy problems. Mike had a video that the blackmailer had sent."

"He never said anything about it to me. Chanse, I don't know what Mike was up to, but I don't know anything about a rich doctor." Glen blew smoke out the window. "He pretty much told me everything, though. I mean, if something like that was going on, he would've told me. He must've been up to something. I mean, come on. Mike loved to rub my face in all the men that wanted him. A rich doctor? I'd have heard all about it."

"He said he was getting the tape on his way to the apartment. I was coming over to look at it when I found him."

Glen shrugged. "Who knows? He must've had a reason for telling you that. Maybe he was trying to get you into his apartment."

"For what?"

Glen laughed. "And into his bed." He stubbed his cigarette out. "Look at the time!" It was starting to get dark outside. "Wanna come back to my place and have a beer?"

"Sure." There was no reason for me not to. Right?

"I just have to make a phone call real quick." He got up and walked over to the phone booth. I watched him walk away. Definitely a nice ass.

I thought about what he had said. The police had found no evidence of a blackmailer in the apartment. Glen didn't know anything about a rich doctor. Yet Mike had told Remy he'd landed someone with more money. What game had Mike been playing? And how had I fit in? Weird.

Glen came back to the table. "Let's go." We walked out of Kaldi's.

It had cooled off as the sun set. A nice breeze was flowing in from the direction of the river as we walked up St. Philip. *I like this guy,* I thought, as Glen started talking about his dreams. He wanted to be a writer, always had, he was saying. He could make me laugh. I felt comfortable with him. More comfortable than I did with Paul. Could Paul make me laugh? I tried to remember. We turned the corner at Dauphine. When we reached the gate that led back to his apartment, he turned and reached up and kissed me again. I slid my arms around him and kissed back.

I heard the sound of a car approaching. It was going pretty slow. I dismissed it as a carload of lost tourists.

The car stopped. I started to turn.

"DIE FAGGOTS!"

There was a bang. A chip of wood splintered off from the gate. There was another bang. I knew that sound. Anyone who'd been a cop knew that sound. I grabbed him and bodily threw him to the sidewalk. "Get down!"

"Ouch!"

There was another bang. I dropped to the sidewalk. "Someone's shooting at us!" I listened for the sound of car doors opening. My heart was pounding in my ears. Then the car shifted into gear, and burned rubber.

I ran out into the street. It was too dark to read the plates. The car was moving away pretty fast. It made a left at Orleans and disappeared. It had been a large dark car. In the twilight it could have been black, navy blue, or green. I didn't know what kind of car it was. An oncoming car honked its horn. I jumped out of the way. I walked back over to the sidewalk. I was starting to shake. I helped Glen to his feet. His face was white. He was gasping for breath. "I don't feel so good."

"We'd better get inside." I was starting to feel a little wobbly. Someone had shot at us.

Glen finally got the gate unlocked. We stepped into the dark hallway. He was shaking, so I put an arm around him. We walked back to the courtyard. He let us into his apartment. He turned on a light. "Oh God, Oh God, Oh God." He picked up a joint. He lit it and took several puffs.

"It's OK." I took the joint from him. I was shaken up myself. No one had shot at me since I left the force. He sat on the couch. I sat beside him. We sat there for a few minutes. "Should we call the police?"

I called Venus. She said she'd be right over. I took the joint and took a long drag. Reeking of marijuana smoke is the last thing I wanted when dealing with the police. But it was keeping me from throwing up.

"People keep telling me the Quarter is dangerous." He put his head in his hands.

"No more so than any other neighborhood in the city." I put the joint out in the ashtray. "I'm going out to wait for Venus. You stay here and relax and try to calm down. Burn some incense." I walked out to the gate. It was swinging back and forth. We hadn't closed it behind us. *That wasn't very safe,* I thought. I shut the gate, and it latched firmly. Maybe Mike hadn't shut the gate properly after he came in. Maybe he hadn't let the killer in. I opened the gate and looked out. There wasn't anyone around. I looked at the front of the gate. There were two holes in the wood. I stepped back inside.

First, a body. Now someone was shooting at me.

Or were they shooting at a faggot?

My mind replayed the entire incident. The slow-moving dark sedan with tinted windows. Glen and I standing in front of the gate. The car slowing down, me starting to turn, the sound of the shots, the wood splintering. Above the engine of the car I'd heard a voice shouting, "Die faggots!"

Or had I? Had it been real? Was I hallucinating?

I shivered again. Maybe the evidence did point to a hate crime. It could've been a hate crime. The message had been there on the wall.

I guess the thing about hate crimes is you know you're different. Gays are not the majority in this country. When you're a kid and you can't figure out why all the other guys are putting up posters of Christie Brinkley or whoever the flavor of the year is, you know you're different. When you start to realize that you're the only boy who thinks it's cool that the Chippendales dancers are on *Oprah,* you know you're different. It's brought home in many ways every day as you get older. You're not only different, you're queer, and that's the lowest of the low. It's the ultimate insult. There's no answer to that when they call you names in the locker room while snapping you with rolled-up damp towels. So, you start to act, you start to pretend. You've learned. Your behavior is not acceptable. So you start hanging the *Sports Illustrated* calendar in your hall locker. You got out for sports and excel, because you can't be a rotten athlete—that would be queer. You lift weights, you jog. You start lying in the showers, talking about having sex with girls, hoping no one else notices your furtive looks at the other boys.

You start getting older. You find out there are others like you. Maybe it's not such an awful thing. You find someone you find attractive, and you try it. It's better than it is with the girls. You want to do it again, and more and more often. You start telling yourself that it's just who you are; you can't help what you are anymore than anyone else can. You start finding meeting places for others like you. You read books about others like you. Maybe it's not that bad. It's just who you are. You start to feel better about it. You start coming out to people you care about. More people know. When they don't care, you feel better and better. Until you get to the point where you don't hide it anymore, and you aren't afraid, and it's OK.

And then you run into something like a dead body with FAGGOTS DIE written in blood above the body.

And suddenly, you don't feel quite so OK anymore.

CHAPTER TWELVE

"I ought to run you in." Venus stood with her hand on her hip, one eyebrow raised. "I ought to run your sorry ass in for obstructing justice."

I was seated on the steps leading to Glen's apartment. I just stared at her. "Huh?"

"Did I or did I not tell you to keep the possibilities of this being a hate crime a secret until I told you different?" Her head was starting to move from side to side. This wasn't a good sign. The hand on the hip was ominous. The head movement was dangerous. "And what do I read in the *TP* this morning over my latte but a story about the latest hate crime in the Quarter." She took a step toward me. "Written by Ms. Paige Tourneur, your pal."

I cursed myself for not reading the paper. I rarely did. I have an aversion to news. Then I cursed Paige. "I didn't tell her, Venus. Please. I'm smarter than that. Would I tell her when I'd be the first person you'd suspect?"

She rolled her eyes. "You could talk your way out of the electric chair."

"Thanks, I think."

She sighed and flipped her notebook shut. She sat down next to me on the steps. "Jarrett Phillips is calling the mayor every hour on the hour demanding that the police find the killer. He's talking to all the local networks, calling the department a bunch of homophobes who don't care about crimes against gays." She looked at me. "Off the record?"

"Yeah." I guess she meant that I couldn't tell Paige. I'm not a reporter.

"They found powder burns on Hansen's fingers and around the entry wound." She looked at me. "He was struggling with his killer."

"But there was no evidence of a struggle." I thought back to his apartment. Everything neat, in its place. Except of course for the body on the floor. "If he'd been fighting over the gun—"

"I don't think this was a hate crime," she said, scratching her forehead. "I think the killer wants us to think it was."

I was relieved to know I wasn't in denial. "But what about tonight?"

"That article in the paper today was bound to rile up some of our finer redneck population. They just weren't smart enough to think about it until someone else brought it up." She laughed. "Thank God this isn't New York or L.A. Could you imagine the rioting and protesters? Thank God this is New Orleans and no one wants to be bothered in the heat."

"I was shot at, Venus."

"By some guys who may or may not have shouted 'Die faggots' as they fired at you—some guys you didn't get a look at, who were in a car you can't identify, with a license plate you didn't see." She shook her head. "I'm sorry, Chanse, but if this happened before this killing would you have thought it was a hate crime?"

I thought about it for a few minutes. "No." I had to admit, I would have thought it was some kids out, drinking too much and thinking that shooting at people was fun. Or a drive-by mistake. What kind of world do we live in anyway?

"Everyone in this city's got hate crime on the brain now." She stood up with a slight groan. "Getting too old for all this running around."

Right. She was in better shape than most men I know. I stood up with her. "All right. Thanks, Venus."

She took my arm. She looked me in the face. "Just be careful, OK? All kinds of things are getting stirred up in this city, and it's awful damned hot. People get crazy in the heat."

"I don't want to live in fear." *Again,* I almost added.

"So don't."

"It's kind of hard with shit like this going down." I walked with her.

"I'll tell you what's hard," she said. "Hard is not being able to drink out of certain water fountains when you're a little girl." She stopped walking when we reached my car. She winked at me. "And now I can't pass one of those fountains without taking a drink from it."

She waved at me as I drove off.

Getting shot at was not one of my favorite things. Danger isn't my middle name.

There were four possibilities. First, it was some crazed redneck homophobe driving through the Quarter with a gun, hoping to shoot some homos. Seeing us kissing was too good to pass up. The second was that it just another random act of violence. Those are becoming more prevalent these days. The third was someone didn't like the questions I was asking about Mike. And the fourth was that there was some kind of cover-up going on, and I was getting in the way.

Yeah. Maybe it was linked to the Kennedy assassinations too.

This is why I don't do murders. The second killing is much easier than the first.

The whole thing was ridiculous, I thought. I wasn't investigating Mike's murder. All I was doing was asking some simple questions. Surely I wasn't asking anything that Venus hadn't asked these same people. I didn't know what kind of progress Venus was making. Maybe that bitchy queen Brian hadn't called her about Remy's threats. She might be rattling different cages than I was.

I walked into the house and checked the machine. Sure enough, it was blinking. The first message was Paige's nightly check-in. The second was from Blaine. It sounded important. But since it was midnight, I decided it could wait until daylight. The third message was from Paul.

Beep. "Chanse, it's me, Paul. I'm in Minneapolis. I hate to do this to you, but I just got off the phone with my mother and I was read the riot act for not having come home since I moved to New Orleans. So after my flights tomorrow, I'm going to fly home to Albuquerque for a few days. I'm sorry, honey, but duty calls. I would much rather be in New Orleans with you. I miss you. I love you. I'll call from Dallas."

I love you.

I froze. Paul had never said those words to me. Did he mean it? Was it just a slip? Was he feeling guilty about going to Dallas? Was he feeling guilty about something else? I got out my cigarettes and lit one. I rewound the message and listened to it again. I hadn't imagined it. He'd said it. Fuck. I rewound it and listened one more time. Damn it, damn it, damn it. I went to bed.

The phone woke me up the next morning at the ungodly hour of 7:30. On the fourth ring I picked it up. "Hello?"

"Make some coffee. I'll stop at Burger King and get some food."

"Blaine?"

"I'm on my way." The phone went dead. What the hell? I started the coffee and brushed my teeth. I didn't get dressed. Blaine has seen me naked before, so seeing me in my underwear wasn't going to upset him. I had just poured myself a second cup of coffee when the doorbell rang. I let him in.

"You look like shit," he said as he set the bag on the coffee table. He was in uniform.

"Fuck you. Coffee's in the kitchen."

He poured himself a cup. He handed me a breakfast sandwich. "Chanse, what the hell is going on?"

"What do you mean?" For a brief moment, I thought he was talking about Paul and me.

"Venus is pissed as all hell at you. She read me the riot act yesterday."

"What for?"

"She thinks you're—and I am quoting—'fucking around in her investigation.'"

"Is that it?" I picked up a greasy hash brown. "She's over it. I saw her last night."

"You did? Why?"

I filled him in on the events of last night.

"What are you doing?" Blaine munched on his own hash brown. "I thought you weren't going to look into this at all."

I explained how Alan and Brian had led me to Remy and Justin. "I told them to contact Venus and talk to her."

"Well, Brian did call her. I don't know what he said, but it pissed her off royally. And if she would have come across Paige yesterday…" Blaine made a slashing movement across his throat. "She's under a lot of pressure from this. Jarrett Phillips is hounding her, and you know he's on the Mayor's Advisory Council, so the mayor's office is putting some pressure on her as well." He picked up his coffee. "You think it was a hate crime?"

"Mike, or last night?"

"Last night."

"Could've been, but I doubt it," I said. "And it makes it hard for me to stay out of it. Now it's personal."

"What do you mean?"

"Someone shot at me last night. Someone tried to kill me. Even if I stop looking into this, they're not going to know that. Now I have to keep looking. I've got to find this guy before he kills me."

"That's assuming that the killer shot at you last night. Christ." Blaine finished his coffee. "I don't like to think that some homophobe shot at you. I don't like to think some homophobe killed Mike."

"Makes you stop and think, doesn't it?" I got up and refilled my coffee cup. "Kind of a weird feeling."

"Yeah." Blaine shivered. "It's weird, you know? I've never really felt any of it on the force, you know? I mean, there are a couple of guys that I know think of me as a faggot, some of the older ex-military ones, but it's just a feeling. No one has ever left notes in my locker, and no one has ever said anything to me. But now, when I walk up on some other cops just hangin' out in the coffee room, they stop talking, like they don't want me to know what they were talking about, you know? And not one of the other cops has asked me what I think. And you know they're talking about it to each other. Even the gay cops aren't talking." He shook his head. "Weird."

He stood. "Gotta go. Be careful, buddy, OK?"

We hugged at the door. "Hey, I don't like this anymore than you do."

"Keep me posted." He did look worried.

"Will do." I shut the door behind him and locked it. I got out the yellow pages. *OK, who's left? Who else was in Mike's life?* I wondered as I started flipping through the pages. Ronnie Bishop, the violent ex. I called, but got his machine. I left a message, stressing the urgency of the call. Then I looked up Jarrett Phillips's office number. I made an appointment to see him that afternoon.

Why is Jarrett Phillips so driven to push the police? I wondered. According to Glen, his relationship with Mike hadn't been much. He was hounding Venus, he was hounding Paige. He was worth talking to.

I called Paige. "Tourneur."

"You got me in some deep shit with Venus."

I could almost hear her smirk. "That's what you get for holding out on me. If you would've told me not to print it, I wouldn't have. You could've told me. You should know that by now."

"I'm sorry, Paige. I wasn't thinking straight. I mean, I was pretty shook up by the whole thing."

"You OK now?"

"Better. I've made some calls to some people that knew Mike."

"Still checking into it?"

"Yeah, I kind of feel like I have to."

"Yeah?" She didn't say anything else. There were some noises from her end, scrambling noises or something. Then I heard her unmistakable, deep, sensuous inhale.

"Are you smoking at your desk?"

"Under my desk, actually." She giggled. "There's no one in my end of the office right now, and I'll just deny it if they smell it later." I pictured it in my head. Paige, under her desk with the telephone. Someone on the far end of the office noticing the rising smoke from under her desk. Someone shouts. Someone else heads for the fire extinguisher. Someone else heads for the fire alarm. It goes off. Paige scrambles out from under her desk, cigarette dangling from her lips, just as they turn on the fire extinguisher.

"Jesus!"

"I suppose you want to know how I found out about the hate-crime angle?"

"Yes." I lit a cigarette of my own.

"You know I can't reveal my sources."

"I won't tell Venus."

"Jarrett Phillips." I could hear her exhale. I pictured the huge cloud of smoke rising up from under her desk. Maybe the sprinkler system would go off.

"How did he know?"

"Don't know. He wouldn't reveal his source, but implied that it was a gay cop on the force."

"You believe him?"

"It's a tough call." I wondered what she was using for an ashtray. Was she catching ashes in the palm of her hand, was she flicking them on the floor, or were they falling into her wastebasket? I pictured an ember igniting a piece of paper in the trash can. Flames leaping up. That would set the sprinklers off. "It's hard to say—I mean, are you gay first or a cop first?"

"Cop. At least I was." I tried to remember when I was on the force. I had never come across a single case involving a gay issue. This was a hard one. Cop first, or gay? If I was on the force and I disagreed with the way Venus was keeping the hate-crime angle a secret, if I felt gays needed to know for their own safety, would I be able to keep my mouth shut? Where do you draw the line? "You have to be a cop first. Otherwise, you won't treat people fairly, and you have to treat everyone the same."

"Yeah."

"I think I'll go over to Jarrett's office this afternoon and see what he knows."

"I'll pray for you to get out before the brainwashing takes hold." Click.

CHAPTER THIRTEEN

Jarrett Phillips's office was on Frenchmen Street in the Faubourg Marigny, the neighborhood on the other side of Esplanade from the Quarter. Paige calls the Marigny the poor man's Quarter: The architecture is much the same, and bars, restaurants, and businesses mix in with private homes. A few years ago the Marigny was dangerous after dark, but then the neighborhood started to make a comeback. Some streets were still unsafe, but for the most part the Marigny was turning into a beautiful place to live.

Jarrett's office was on Washington Park. The building was a double camelback. Jarrett lived in half of the bottom and the upstairs. The other half served as the office for Gay Rights Now! I'd never been to his office. The house looked beautiful from the outside. The emerald-green paint looked fresh enough to still smell new. The lawn was immaculate. In the driveway beside the house sat a sky-blue Miata convertible with a vanity plate that read GAYRITZ. I'm sure it stood for Gay Rights. I'm sure most people thought it said Gay Ritz. From the looks of the house, they wouldn't be far off.

I walked up the steps. I rang the doorbell on the left side. Most camelbacks were based on the right side. "Yes?" a voice came out of the intercom next to the bell.

"Chanse MacLeod. I have a 2 o'clock appointment."

"I'll buzz you in."

There was a buzz. I pushed. I stepped into a room almost the temperature of my refrigerator. It was painted deep royal blue. Several black-and-white prints of artistic male and female nudes hung on the walls. I don't think I would've gone with that kind of art choice for a gay non-profit. Then again, it wasn't my office. There were a couple of file cabinets, an overstuffed sofa that matched the walls, a glass and brass coffee table, and a huge oak desk. On a credenza behind the desk was a coffeemaker. A woman wearing khaki slacks, a black silk blouse open to show cleavage, and heels came around the desk. She wore dangling jet-black earrings to match her jet-black hair, which was immaculately styled. She looked to be about 5 foot 10. She reached up to kiss my cheek.

"It's good to see you again, Chanse." She smiled. Pearly white teeth flashed.

"Yvonne?"

She danced around in a circle. "I clean up pretty good, don't I?"

I'd never known her last name. She was a lesbian who bartended at the Pub on weekends. I'd never seen her in anything except a sleeveless Pub T-shirt and cutoffs. She was one of the best bartenders in the Quarter. "You not slinging cocktails anymore?"

"On the weekends," she said. "Can't give up that money. But I believe in what we're doing here." She grinned. "Pay's not bad either. I'll tell Jarrett you're here." She went through a door.

I picked up a copy of *The Advocate*. Another straight movie star playing gay onscreen was on the cover. Big deal. Like we have two heads or something. Like playing gay was such a huge acting challenge. Nobody makes a big deal out of it when someone plays a serial killer. Whatever. I tossed the magazine back on the table and picked up the *International Male* catalog. I turned a few pages. Where do they find these guys?

The door opened. "Chanse!" Jarrett Phillips came toward me, his hand outstretched. "So glad to see you."

I shook his hand. I didn't like him. He was about 5 foot 10. His body looked naturally lean but seemed to have gone soft as he'd gotten older. His blond hair was combed carefully to cover a bald spot. Not carefully enough—I could see it. He was wearing a navy-blue blazer with gold buttons, a pink Tommy Hilfiger shirt, khaki slacks, and a pair of tan deck shoes. Perfectly preppy. His blue eyes looked me up and down behind wire-rimmed glasses. His smile was too big to be real. He'd probably been rush chairman at his fraternity. His grip was firm.

"Shall we go into my office?"

I followed him. A much bigger oak desk was in there. Several leather chairs were strategically placed in front of it for guests. A huge oak armoire graced one wall. There were framed photographs all over the walls. I glanced at one and was impressed. It showed Jarrett shaking hands with a former governor of Louisiana—one who had never been tried for a crime: That was rare. The other pictures showed Jarrett with the mayor, several gay celebrities, and then there was a studio portrait of Jarrett. He looked a lot younger. It was black-and-white, a head shot. White-blond hair hung to his shoulders. No glasses. He looked good.

He noticed me looking. "A holdover from my modeling days. I never made it big, but I managed to get by."

"Ever pose nude?"

He looked appalled. "Of course not!"

Interesting. I bit. "Why not?"

He sat down in his chair and leaned back. "I knew I was destined for great things, and I didn't want that sort of thing to bite me in the ass."

I sat down and crossed my legs. "Great things?"

"Like this." He waved around the room. "Doing great work for the community. Could you imagine what the Christians would say if nude photos of me turned up?"

"I guess it would confirm their opinion that we're all godless perverts."

"Exactly." He narrowed his eyes. "We're doing great work here, Chanse, great work. My goal is to have total equality for gays in Louisiana in four years."

"And then?"

"Then we go national." He grinned. "I would be lying if I didn't see a future in politics for myself."

Good luck, I thought. Somehow, I didn't see the straight masses rushing to the polls to vote for him, or any gay man. Despite its liberal reputation, New Orleans was a conservative city. In the Quarter anything went, but the rest of the city was an enclave of conservatism. I couldn't see white-glove fund-raisers for a homo being held in a stately Garden District mansion. Uptown either. What the hell, let him dream.

"So, what kind of volunteer work are you interested in?" he went on.

"Volunteer work?"

"Isn't that why you're here?" He beamed at me. "I must say I'm very pleased. I have to say that when we met at that fund-raiser at the Johnson-Buchmaiers', I thought you were remarkably unconcerned about the situation we gays find ourselves in today in our so-called free society. Oppression is everywhere we turn. For every step forward, there's always some fascist judge ready to slap us back two. I am always amazed that supposedly impartial judges, sworn to uphold the Constitution, can be so easily swayed in attempting to legislate morality. As if this were a theocratic state!"

"Actually," I uncrossed my legs, "I'm here to talk about Mike Hansen."

The smile left his face. "Another innocent victim of the oppressors."

"You're awfully interested in his murder."

"It's a justifiable concern." Jarrett took out a handkerchief and mopped off his face. "Do you know the statistics on hate crimes in this city? The police look the other way while we're robbed, beaten, and murdered. Instead of trying to track down the real criminals, they raid our bars and try to put them out of business. You're damned right I'm interested in his murder. I intend to keep pressuring the police until they do something about it!"

"So your only interest is to make sure his killer is brought to justice?"

"What other interest could I have?" He stared at me. "Do you feel safe walking the streets knowing that some maniac is out there killing gays? You saw the message on his wall firsthand."

I chose to ignore that. I didn't need to replay the image in my head. "I have it on good authority that you were personally involved with him."

The eyes narrowed. "Who told you that?"

"Does it matter?"

He leaned back again, drumming his fingers together. "He was a beautiful man."

"No argument there."

"I met him at a fund-raiser for my organization. It was at the Buchmaier mansion on State Street." Jarrett's eyes narrowed. "He was interested in our cause."

Somehow I doubted that. "Interesting."

"He wanted to volunteer. I talked to him briefly at the party and gave him my card. He called me the next week and we met for dinner."

And no doubt you paid, I thought. "So did he become involved as a volunteer?"

"Yes, but not as a standard volunteer, making calls and things like that. Mike was more important than that."

I was willing to bet that Jarrett never said something like that to his other volunteers. "And just how important was he?"

"Is this necessary?"

"You can talk to me, or you can talk to the police," I said.

"I'll take my chances."

"OK, then." I switched gears. "So you and Mike weren't involved personally?"

"We had dinner a few times," Jarrett said. "I liked him. He was intelligent, if naive. I think I was the first person who appreciated him as more than just a pretty face, and he liked that. Just like so many unfortunates in our community, most people treated him as a sex object."

"Did Mike ever talk to you about people he was seeing?"

"Mike was sexually active, if that's what you're trying to get me to say." His face started to flush. "I don't see how any of this is important. The poor man was murdered before he could begin to develop his potential." His voice was getting louder. "And you a gay man! You should be ashamed of yourself, digging into his sex life like this. Why aren't you out there finding out who really killed him? Or are you just looking for dirt?"

I controlled my temper. "It's possible that whoever killed him was someone he knew."

"It was a political murder!" He slammed his hands down on his desk. "You saw it, didn't you? 'Faggots die,' isn't that what it said?"

I stared at him for a minute. His source in the department was a good one. "I don't think it was a hate crime, Jarrett, and neither do the police."

"That's a good one." He laughed. "How typical. Sweep it under the rug, blame the victim—isn't that where this is all heading?"

"Knock it off, Jarrett." I kept my voice quiet. "I believe he was murdered by someone he knew."

His eyes narrowed. "You're a traitor to your own kind. You're just like the police. If a gay man is killed, it's got to be a sex crime of some sort. Mike was sexually active, so he asked for it—isn't that what you think? What you believe? You're a straight homophobe trapped in a gay body." He smiled at me. "You should get help, Mr. MacLeod. Why do you hate being gay?"

I bit my lip and counted to 10. I wanted to throttle the smug bastard. I stood. "I don't hate being gay. I only hate people who might have information that could help bring a killer to justice but are too busy screaming 'hate crime' to do anything about it. You know what I think, Jarrett? I think you don't give a damn who killed Mike. I think you're glad he was killed so you can use it to further your own agenda."

"Get out of my office!" Spittle sprayed from his lips.

"Gladly." I walked to the door. I looked back at him. He was holding a paperweight in the shape of a pink triangle. "Mike was a person, Jarrett. He wasn't a martyr for your cause."

"Get out!" The paperweight flew. I ducked. It shattered against the wall, spewing shards of pink glass all over me. I walked out the door.

I stood in the outer office for a moment and took a deep breath. Yvonne's eyes were wide open. "You must've really pissed him off."

I walked over to her desk. "He's trying to turn this whole Mike Hansen murder into a crusade, and it's wrong."

"I'll walk you out." Once outside, she said, "Mike's murder shook Jarrett up. A lot. He thinks it's somehow related to GRN."

"He's crazy."

"He's a good man, Chanse. We do good work here. Don't be so quick to judge." She crossed her arms. "And you can't deny the message the killer left. 'Faggots die,' right?"

"Right."

"One of my brothers was killed by homophobes." Yvonne stared out at the park. A young man with no shirt on was playing Frisbee with his dog. "We're from Mississippi, my family. I mean, I'm a dyke, and I have a gay brother. He decided to come out right after he got out of high school, and our little Christian town went nuts. One night a bunch of drunk rednecks jumped my brother. They beat him to death." She looked back at me. "But they got the wrong brother. Instead of my gay brother, David, they killed my brother Steve. Steve was straight and only 17. And you know what? The killers walked. In Mississippi it's OK to kill gays. All you've got to do is say they made a pass at you. When I turned 18, I got the hell out of that miserable town. I'll never go back. Ever."

"I'm sorry, Yvonne."

"It's OK," she said. "That's why I work here. I have to do something to stop things like that from happening to someone else. No one deserves to die because of who they are."

"You're right."

"Are you coming to the vigil tomorrow night?"

I stared at her. "Vigil?"

She stepped back into the office and handed me a flyer. It announced, on bright pink paper, a candlelight vigil in Jackson Square the following evening in memory of Mike Hansen. Mike Hansen: hate-crime victim. I put it in my pocket. "Thanks. Yvonne, I don't think it was a hate crime."

"What about the message on the wall?"

"I think the killer did that to make it look like a hate crime."

"You know, you might want to try to find out who Mike's last lover was." Her left eye closed in a wink. "Mike talked to me sometimes when I was at work at the bar. He thought he'd hit the jackpot."

"Yeah?"

Yvonne shrugged. "Never told me a name. All I know is it was someone in Uptown, in the closet, with a lot of money. Maybe he didn't want to come out of the closet." She turned to go back inside. "Oh, Mike said he was a King of Rex."

I watched the door shut behind her.

The Uptown rich man again. The blackmail victim. I had the feeling there was a lot more to this whole thing. Maybe Mike's last lover had some of the answers for me.

A King of Rex, huh? I smiled to myself. That shouldn't be too hard to track down.

CHAPTER FOURTEEN

How sad that the future of the gay community rested in the hands of a slime like Jarrett Phillips. I shook my head as I opened my car door and got inside. My next car would not have black vinyl interior. It should be against the law to sell cars like that in the South. I started the car and drove home. Twenty minutes later I was finally in the cool of my apartment. Thank God. My electric bill was going to be outrageous, but it was worth every penny. I got a Dr. Pepper out of the refrigerator. The red light on the answering machine was blinking. I hit the playback button with a sigh.

Beep. "Hi, Chanse. I know you said you'd call, but I'm impatient. This is Glen, by the way. I just wanted to call and see how you were doing. I wish I could say that I was doing well, but my downstairs neighbor has been murdered, and I was shot at last night, and then I look at yesterday's paper and see that Mike's death was a hate crime, and now I'm, like, afraid to leave my apartment. Maybe I should just move, get a transfer, and get out of here. I always thought New Orleans was a cool place to live, but now I'm not so sure. I had fun yesterday—I mean, until we got shot at—and maybe we could get together sometime? Have a nice day, bye."

I popped the top of my Dr. Pepper can and took a long swig. I wiped the sweat off my forehead with a paper towel. I called Glen back and left a short message on his machine.

It probably wasn't the brightest thing in the world to do. Who was I hurting by seeing Glen again? Paul was on his way to Albuquerque to spend time with his parents, and then he's off flying the friendly skies again.

Air mattress, air mattress.

Was that fair? He said in his message that he loved me. That was a new development. One that we definitely needed to talk about.

I sighed and called Paige. "Hey, girl, look something up for me?"

She sighed. "What now?"

"Can you find out for me who the last 15 Kings of Rex were?" I doubted Mike's lover would have ruled Rex earlier than that. "And which of them were doctors?"

"Mike's lover?"

"Possibly." I told her what Yvonne said.

"I'll call you back."

I changed into workout clothes. Might as well head down to Bodytech and get my workout in. I knew I should call Venus, but I wasn't in the mood. She could be a royal bitch when she wanted to be. She'd been pretty cool about me poking around in her investigation so far. I don't think she'd have been thrilled to know that I'd seen Jarrett. I packed my bag, grabbed my keys, and headed back out into the oven.

The parking lot at Bodytech had a couple of cars in it. I figured I'd be the only idiot who'd be working out in the heat. Alan smiled at me from behind the desk. "Hey, Chanse. Kind of late in the day for you, isn't it? Long night?" His eyebrows went up. I could tell what he was thinking: *Paul's out of town, so what were you up to last night?*

I wasn't about to tell him that I'd been shot at. He shrugged when he realized I wasn't saying any more. "Did you see Justin and Remy?" he asked as he got me a locker key.

"Yeah. Nice guys."

"You think one of them killed Mike?"

"Anything's possible."

"Was it really a hate crime?"

I shrugged. I wasn't getting into this with yet another person.

"Someone threw red paint all over the front doors last night and wrote 'Die faggots' in the paint." Alan shivered. "What's going on, Chanse?"

I didn't know what to say.

Alan motioned for me to lean over the counter. "The ex is here."

"The ex?"

"The ex! The ex! Ronnie Bishop!"

The ex who hadn't returned my phone call. I followed Alan's gaze. Sure enough, standing in front of a mirror doing curls with a pair of dumbbells was Ronnie Bishop. "Thanks." I changed and walked out to the gym floor.

I knew Ronnie Bishop slightly. When I first moved to New Orleans and joined the force, he'd been living with a police detective named Gilbert Robideaux. They'd been together a few years. Blaine had filled me in on them. Apparently, Gilbert didn't want a monogamous relationship. Ronnie did. Gilbert was winning the battle of wills. At first I felt sorry for Ronnie. It would suck, I'd thought, to love someone who wanted to keep sleeping around. My pity gradually turned into contempt. Why would anyone put up with that? I'd have thrown Gilbert out on his sorry ass.

Plus, Gilbert wasn't exactly a dreamboat. He was short, dumpy, had bad teeth, and was a racist to boot. Not exactly someone to write home about. The only things I ever heard Gilbert say about Ronnie weren't nice either. After a while, Gilbert moved in with a florist with a successful shop in Uptown. They were still together and completely monogamous. That had to hurt.

I walked over to where Ronnie was working out. He was about an inch or so over six feet tall. His thick white-blond hair, dark underneath, was immaculately styled, as always—he knew it was his best feature. He was lanky, and his skin was reddish gold. At first glance he looked attractive, although the hair was a little distracting. You noticed the flaws only when you saw him up close. The lines around his mouth and eyes became more apparent, and his face was long and thin. Two blue eyes were set close together at the top of a narrow beak of a nose. His lips were narrow too, almost nonexistent. He'd probably been bone thin in high school, but years of working out had made his shoulders broad and firmly muscled. The biceps he was working were thick. But the legs sticking out from the green cotton shorts were thin. Muscled but thin—far too thin for his strongly muscled upper body. Obviously, his sole purpose in working out always had been to look good in bars—from the waist up.

He set the weights down. "Hello, Chanse." His voice was raspy, scratchy, as if someone had taken a Brillo pad to his vocal cords.

"Why didn't you call me back?"

"I got better things to do with my time than worry about who killed Mike." He folded his arms. I got a better look at the strong pecs beneath his green tank top. "I'm surprised it took this long."

I raised my eyebrows. "Really?"

"Save it for someone else." He scowled at me. "Mike and I've been over since Mardi Gras, OK?"

"And you were OK with that?"

"Did I have a choice?"

"You always have a choice."

"You didn't know Mike." He laughed. "You want to talk to me about Mike? OK. Buy me an early dinner, and I'll fill you in on all the gory details." He picked up the weights.

"OK." I started my own workout. There probably wasn't much he could tell me that would be of any use to me at this point—if he was telling the truth. He was the last person in the world I wanted to spend money on, but I was also getting curious. Nobody I'd talked to thus far had anything nice to say about Mike. I doubted that Ronnie would be the first. Mike had burned a lot of people. He'd burned Ronnie the worst. He'd probably been through the wringer with Venus already. She can be a real bitch when she wants to be.

I cut my workout short so he wouldn't have to wait for me. I noticed something odd about him. While undressing, he wrapped his towel around his waist before taking off his underwear. Very weird. I just peel off everything and walk stark naked to the shower. Most people do. Whatever. Maybe he was afraid that the sight of his ass would be too tempting for me.

In his dreams.

We decided on Semolina's on Magazine Street. We were the only people there. The waiter was a cute boy with olive skin and green eyes. Ronnie's eyes followed him around as he got our iced tea and a plate of bread. Semolina's has the best garlic butter I've ever tasted. I could easily eat an entire loaf spread with it.

"Like him?" I asked as Ronnie watched him take our orders into the kitchen.

"Hot, but too young." Ronnie took a swig of tea. "No more boys in their 20s for me."

I hate myself when I think bitchy thoughts. I try not to do it. The problem is that sometimes they don't stay in your mind where they belong. I had to bite my lip.

"I can still get boys in their 20s," he said, squeezing his lemon.

It was creepy. Surely he wasn't psychic.

"What did you want to know about me and Mike?" He added Sweet'N Low to his tea. "I already talked to the police."

"Did he tell you about this rich boyfriend he had?"

Ronnie laughed. "Where did you hear that stupid story?"

"Mike."

He rolled his eyes. "Mike was always a drama queen. He lived for drama. If it didn't happen he invented it. Very simple."

"You don't think it was true?"

"He was a liar, Chanse. Mike wanted out of our relationship, but he didn't want me out of his life. He called me every week. He wanted us to stay friends. What he really wanted was to let me know how many men he was fucking, the prick."

"He'd do that?"

"Of course. Another of his little games," Ronnie said.

"One thing he hated more than anything was for someone he'd slept with to be with anyone else. About a month or two after we broke up, I started dating a DJ at Oz. Nothing serious. Just dinner a couple of times. One night we went dancing at Oz. Mike saw us there. The next day he calls me up and says he still loves me." Ronnie picked up a piece of bread. "I told him he was nuts. The next thing I know he's at my front door. We wound up in bed. He says he wants to get back with me, that he's sorry he left me, all that shit. It was all shit. Once I broke up with Geoff, he changed his mind again."

"Geoff?"

"Geoff Rivers. The DJ."

I didn't know him.

"As soon as he's fucked things up for me, he's out of my life again."

"So why didn't you start seeing Geoff again?"

"He was pissed at me for breaking up with him," Ronnie said. "Can't blame him."

"Was Mike faithful when you were together?"

"No more than Gilbert was."

The waiter put our salads in front of us. Ronnie smiled at him when their eyes met.

"You remember Gilbert, don't you, Chanse?"

"Yes." Ronnie thought I'd slept with Gilbert when they were together.

"Mike wanted it all. He wanted money, a nice house. I went broke fixing up my place for him. New furniture, renovations, everything. But when someone with more money came along, he was gone, leaving me with a stack of unpaid bills that'll take years to pay."

"Someone with more money?"

"Story of his life," Ronnie said. "When a bigger and better deal came along, he was gone. That's how he came here in the first place. He was from some backwoods place in North Alabama, some little rural area where everyone's a religious maniac. He told me his parents' church was one step above handling snakes. He moved to Birmingham when he was 18 and started working at a health club. He started seeing some guy who worked for the Birmingham paper, and they were together for a couple of years. Then he won the Mr. Hot Birmingham contest. You know what that is?"

"No."

"Not a circuit boy, are you?"

"No."

"Mr. Hot Birmingham is a preliminary contest for Mr. Hotlanta, which is held during Hotlanta weekend."

That I had heard of. Hotlanta weekend is one of the major circuit events of the year. It drew thousands of gay men from all over the country to party, do lots of drugs, and hang out with other circuit boys.

"When he was in Atlanta, he met a guy from New Orleans. Do you know Lenny Bertolucci?"

"Only by sight." Lenny Bertolucci was one of the most beautiful men in New Orleans. He had olive skin and blue-black hair. His body looked like he spent three hours a day in the gym.

"Lenny was Mike's first victim in New Orleans. They met, and before long Mike was coming to New Orleans every other weekend. He left the guy in Birmingham and moved down here to be with Lenny."

"He told me the guy in Birmingham threw him out."

"Maybe," Ronnie said. "Probably got tired of Mike coming down here and slipping that big dick to Lenny. I don't know. Lenny and Mike didn't last long. Mike met me."

"Love at first sight?"

"That's what I thought." Ronnie was bypassing the garlic butter that I was consuming by the spoonful. Fine. More for me. "Turns out I make more money than Lenny, which was part of it," he said. "Mike loved me, though, I know it. If I'd had more money, he wouldn't have left me."

Yeah, that's love. "Mike told me he left you because you were violent."

"Good story." Ronnie laughed. "No, he left because he found his next pigeon."

"The rich guy?"

"No one's told you about Mike's doctor?" Ronnie's eyebrows went up. "As soon as he found his bigger and better deal, he was gone. Some doctor in Uptown, in the closet, with a wife and kids. I never knew his name. He was going to pay for Mike to go back to school and get a degree. When he divorced his wife, Mike was going to live in a great big mansion in Uptown. Mike was proud of himself."

"I thought you said he lied to me about that."

"Yeah, well." He shrugged. "Mike lied about a lot of things. I don't know for sure that this was true."

"You never knew the name?"

He shook his head, tossing his hair. He did that a lot. "Nope. Old Family Money. The guy had been in the closet all of his life. Afraid of losing his inheritance. Married, kids, the whole ball of wax. But he was going to divorce his wife and have Mike move in. Mike was never going to have to work another day in his life. Mike wouldn't tell me his name, because he was afraid I'd fuck it up for him some-how, like maybe I'd out the guy or something. He just had Remy on the side in case something went wrong with the doctor," he said. "Believe it or not."

"Would you have outed the guy?"

Ronnie bared his teeth in a smile. "Would you?"

"Probably not."

"Have you ever been in love?"

"Once. A long time ago."

"I loved Mike, Chanse. I wanted to spend my life with him. When I found out he was cheating on me, I wanted to die. I wanted to kill myself. When he left me, I was sick for months. I lost 20 pounds. I couldn't eat, I couldn't sleep, and then when I'd start to get over him, he'd waltz back into my life and fuck me over again."

"Did you want to kill him?"

Ronnie stared into his glass of iced tea. "No, I never wanted to kill him."

"How did you feel when you found out he was dead?"

"I cried." He stirred the tea with his straw. His eyes were getting wet. "I didn't want him dead, Chanse. And what was worse was that his death set me free. The pain was over. He wasn't coming back again. I hoped he would, you know. Every time he'd come back, I wanted it to be for good. I prayed for it. I wished for it. But it's not going to happen now. So I can move on." Ronnie wiped at his eyes. "I just wish he didn't have to die."

I didn't know what to say. I wasn't sure if I should pat his hand, make sympathetic noises. So I just sat there.

He stood. "I can't stay. I'm sorry." He walked out of the restaurant.

The waiter came up with two plates of Shrimp Roban in his hands. He looked confused. "The food—"

"Box it up to go, please. My friend had to leave."

I paid the bill while I waited for the two boxes of steaming hot food.

Thank God Paige likes Shrimp Roban.

CHAPTER FIFTEEN

I decided to drive over to Paige's to see if she was home from work yet. The smell of the Shrimp Roban in the car was making my stomach growl. I was going to sit in the driveway and eat mine out of the carton if she wasn't home.

I was starving.

Paige rented a carriage house from an elderly Jewish widow. The main house was huge. It was just a few houses past where Carondelet crossed State Street. State Street was where some of the wealthier people of New Orleans lived. Paige's Honda Civic was parked on the street. That was unusual. Paige always parked in the driveway. Being a crime reporter hadn't hardened Paige. Instead, it made her fearful for her own safety. She had never said anything to me about it, but witnessing the killing of that store clerk had terrified her. There'd been several robberies and muggings in her neighborhood. She carried a gun with her everywhere now.

I parked on the street. I walked up the driveway. Mrs. Bloomberg was picking roses on the side of the house. She was barely five feet tall, and very round. Paige once said that if Mrs. Bloomberg laid down on her side, she would roll like a tire all the way down State Street to the river. "A little hot to be in the garden today, Mrs. Bloomberg."

She straightened up. She was wearing a cotton sleeveless

housedress and a sun hat. She cracked her back. She sniffed at me. "You kids are so spoiled by air-conditioning. You don't know what hot is."

"Very true, Mrs. Bloomberg."

"The only reason I run mine is to keep the damp out of the house." She cut another stem. "Tired of having to have people come out and rehang my damned wall paper."

I headed back around to the carriage house. It was small but cozy. It was painted gray with yellow trim. I rang the doorbell. I could hear Paige moving around inside. The door opened. Her hair was mussed, her makeup in ruins.

"I don't know who the kings are yet," she said.

Oops, I thought. "Bad time?"

Paige laughed. "Is there ever a good time? Get out of the heat, for God's sake."

I walked inside. The carriage house was divided into a bedroom, bathroom, a kitchenette, and one big room that doubled as dining/living room. Paige had painted the big room a soothing blue. Her curtains were gold, with blue sashes. The floor was hardwood. She always complained about keeping it clean. It was almost Spartan in the lack of furniture. Most of it she'd picked up at thrift shops. Her bookcases were overflowing, and stacks of books lay all over the place. I could see her computer was on. "Were you working on *Belle?*"

"Trying to." She eyed the bag. "That smells good."

"Shrimp Roban from Semolina's." I handed her the bag. She carried it into the kitchen. She got down two plates and two wineglasses.

"To what do I owe this incredible honor?"

"Ronnie Bishop walked out on dinner because he couldn't

talk about Mike anymore." I watched her fill the glasses with red wine.

She emptied the cartons of food onto the plates. "I can top that. I got to talk to Mike's mother today." She rolled her eyes at me. "You know, my mom is no prize, but all I could think about when talking to this woman was how horrible it would've been to be her child."

"Ronnie said Mike was from rural Alabama."

"You don't even begin to comprehend how rural until you talk to this woman." Paige handed me a plate and glass. "She's prayed for Mike every day since he revealed his sin to her. She's prayed for him to see the light of our Lord Jesus and be saved, and she will pray every day from now until she dies that our Lord Jesus will find it in his heart to forgive Mike for his sinful life."

"Charming."

"She even quoted some Bible verses at me." Paige shuddered. "Just what I needed to hear. I was tempted to tell her I'm a lesbian just to shut her up."

"Why were you talking to her?"

"I didn't want to." Paige put a spoonful of Shrimp Roban into her mouth and moaned with pleasure. "She came down to the paper and found me. She's in town to claim the body and take it back to Alabama for 'proper Christian burial.' She read some of the stuff I'd written in the paper about Mike and wanted to straighten me out on a few things."

"Like what?"

"That Mike had been raised a good Christian, and that it wasn't his family's fault that he turned his back on God and ran off to the evil big city to live a life of sin." Paige sipped her wine. "My God, he must have run for his life!

After I was finished with her, I knocked off early. I'd had enough hate and intolerance for one day, thank you very much."

I filled her in on my talk with Ronnie Bishop. "So when he left, I had the food boxed up and took a chance that you might have left early."

"Usually a safe bet." Paige grinned at me. "Boy, did I get in trouble for smoking at my desk!"

"They're going to fire you someday."

"I wish they would. It'd be the biggest favor they could do me," she said. "So do you think Ronnie could be our killer?"

"I don't think so." I mopped up the sauce with a piece of bread. "I mean, I believe that he could kill Mike, and probably had moments when he wanted to. But it would've been done in the heat of the moment. He doesn't strike me as the type who'd try to make it look like a hate crime. I mean, that took a certain amount of cunning."

"And he isn't cunning enough?"

"I don't think so." I refilled our wineglasses. "Like I said, he'd have killed him in the heat of the moment. I can't see him planning it out. I don't think his mind works that way. If he'd have done it, he'd have probably stayed there crying until the police came."

"Did you know him before?"

"Slightly. Not well." I thought about the confrontation we'd had three years earlier in the Pub. Ronnie had been convinced that I was having an affair with Gilbert. He'd tried to punch me. I'd thrown him out of the bar into Bourbon Street. No, I couldn't see him planning it out. "I don't think it was him."

"Well, if it wasn't a hate crime, who could it have been?"

Paige leaned back in her chair. "I've done a little checking on our friend Jarrett Phillips." She retrieved a file from her desk. "I had the morgue dig this stuff up."

I opened the folder and looked at a stack of photocopied newspaper articles. "This much coverage in the paper on Jarrett?"

She nodded. "When he started Gay Rights Now! he got a lot of coverage. Did you know that he used to be a model?"

"Yeah. He told me."

"He did pretty well for himself. He was no supermodel, but he did OK. He's originally from Mississippi. Hattiesburg. He went to Ole Miss, where he was a Kappa Sigma, a cheerleader, and active in school politics."

"Big surprise there."

"He went to Fort Lauderdale for spring break one year, and that's where he was 'discovered,'" Paige said. "His senior year he took a lot of trips to New York for modeling shoots. After he graduated, he moved up there and started working. He came out while he was in New York, and became an activist. When he got too old to model, he moved here and started Gay Rights Now! with his own money."

"Why here?"

"He said that he'd always loved New Orleans and wanted to live here. And since Louisiana still had a sodomy law on the books, he decided to start his work here."

"Interesting."

"Even more interesting is this." Paige grinned at me. "After a year, his little organization was completely broke. He went through his money fast, and GRN was having trouble finding funding. Then, about three years ago, after barely surviving for two years, everything changed. GRN started getting lots of anonymous donations. Large sums. Last year they got over a million dollars in anonymous donations. Doesn't that strike you as odd? I mean, a million dollars anonymously? That's a lot of money. GRN does a lot of fund-raisers at private homes, like your friend Allan Johnson's, and sometimes at bars and things, but they don't raise nearly as much money as they get in the anonymous donations."

"That's weird."

"Doesn't make sense, does it?"

"No."

Paige got the wine bottle. "Get this. Do you know Mitchell Craig?"

The name was familiar, but I couldn't place it. "Should I?"

"City Council? He's been on it forever."

"OK."

"Well, while I wouldn't exactly call him a homophobe, over the years he's always voted against gays whenever an issue came up. Always. Then around the time all the anonymous donations started coming in, he started voting for gays." She leaned back in her chair and smiled at me. "Isn't it kind of odd that someone who was always antigay suddenly changed to progay?"

"Maybe he has a kid that came out."

She shook her head. "No kids. And it happened right around the same time anonymous donations began to pour into GRN."

"Blackmail," I said. Mike's lover was closeted. There were lots of closeted, married gay men in New Orleans. Lots. My landlady, Barbara, was always trying to fix me up with some closeted married friend of hers.

"Exactly what I was thinking." She grinned at me. "At first, I thought I was just projecting, because I don't like Jarrett, but it looks likely the more I think about it. He's getting his anonymous donations through blackmail."

"That may be." I thought some more. "But it's not a motive to kill Mike."

"Maybe Mike was bait." Paige took her plate into the kitchen. "He was hot, remember? What gay man wouldn't want him? Maybe he was in on it, for a cut. He would lure the men in, take pictures or videotapes, and then the blackmail would start. But maybe with this doctor guy, Mike decided to play for keeps."

"Then why hire me?"

"To scare Jarrett into leaving the doctor alone." Paige refilled her glass. "You said yourself that Jarrett showed up at Mike's apartment. Maybe he'd already been there."

It made sense. "That would explain me being shot at. But how did they know when I'd be walking along Dauphine?"

"Maybe it was unrelated," Paige said. "Jarrett is milking this whole 'hate crime' thing for all it's worth. Wouldn't it be ironic if he turned out to be the killer?"

"Very."

"You didn't bring your pot along, did you?" She looked at me hopefully.

I shook my head. "I didn't know I was coming here when I left the house. You want to go over to my place?"

"OK. I'll follow you."

It was dark when I pulled up in front of my house. Paige pulled in behind me. I parked in front so Paige wouldn't have wait outside while I went through the whole house. We climbed the steps together. I put my keys into the lock.

"Porch light must be blown." I frowned as I turned the key. I swung open the door and stepped aside to let Paige go past.

There was a bang. Paige screamed. Another bang. A burst of light from near the kitchen. I shoved Paige down. The bullet sank into the living room wall. I heard a crash as Paige fell over the love seat. I crouched down. I could barely make out the form of someone moving slowly into the living room from the hall area. *Fuck,* I thought, searching fruitlessly for Paige's purse with her gun in it. I could hear her moaning.

The form came closer. I moved away from the door. The damned streetlight was casting too much light. I crawled along the front of the couch. When I was close enough, I sprang.

We crashed back into one of my bookcases. Books came tumbling down. One hit me on the head and dazed me. The intruder shoved me away. I grabbed hold of his shirt. He smacked me in the head with the gun. Dazed, I fell backwards onto a pile of books. I hung on to the shirt. There was a ripping sound.

Paige screamed again.

He ran out the front door.

I started after him but changed my mind. I wasn't armed, he was. I had to make sure Paige was OK. I switched on the living room light. The room was trashed. Paige was lying on the floor holding her arm. I could see blood coming through her fingers. I looked at my hand. I was holding a piece of a shirt, a black cotton button-down.

"Are you OK?" I knelt beside her.

She nodded, her face white. "It hurts."

I called 911.

CHAPTER SIXTEEN

"I don't need to go to the hospital," Paige said as the paramedic cleaned her arm. The bullet had just grazed her.

"You need to have a tetanus shot," the paramedic replied. "You were lucky."

"Tell me about it," she said. While waiting for the paramedics and the police, she'd alternated between tears and anger.

I finished giving my statement to the patrol officer. The plastic bag of pot was burning a hole in my pocket. All I needed was for the police to go through my house and come across my stash. Venus had been cool so far, but I didn't want to push my luck. She'd lost a younger brother to a heroin overdose when she was a teenager. She gave anti-drug talks at schools. I heard a car pull up outside and walked out onto the porch.

It was Venus. She didn't look happy. Probably interrupted her dinner or something. "Do you have to call me every time something happens in your life, MacLeod?" she said as she opened the gate.

I shrugged. "It's your investigation."

"And what makes you think this has anything to do with my investigation?" She put a hand on her hip and started tapping her foot. She was wearing a yellow silk blouse and a tight navy-blue skirt, stockings and heels.

Uh-oh, I thought. "Hope I didn't interrupt anything important."

"I was having dinner with a man that I've been hoping would ask me out for the last year." Her eyebrows went up. "Start talking." So much for her being a lesbian.

I gave her the thumbnail sketch of what had happened.

"That's it?" She looked like she could easily kill me.

"Look, my client is murdered on Monday, I'm shot at on Wednesday, and on Thursday someone breaks into my house and shoots my best friend. You think these are all isolated incidents? Nobody's that unlucky."

"True." She made a face as I lit a cigarette. "I don't know, Chanse. What the hell have you been up to? Who are you making nervous?"

I shrugged. "Jarrett Phillips, maybe."

"Something about him rubs me the wrong way," she said, watching me smoking with the look of someone who's just quit. I thought about offering her one, but decided it would be better not to. "You think Jarrett broke into your house and shot at you?"

"No. It wasn't Jarrett. I mean, I wasn't able to get a look at the guy at all. It was dark, and he was wearing a mask of some sort. But the body type was different. Jarrett's maybe 5 foot 8. This guy was taller."

"Shame you didn't get a good look at him," Venus said. She pulled out her cell phone. "Did the patrol officer call for the crime scene unit?"

"I think so."

"Well, how the hell did I get here first?" She punched numbers into her cell phone. "Get me that piece of shirt you tore off the guy. I want a look at it."

Obediently, I went back into the apartment. Paige was still arguing with the paramedic, but it looked like flirting. I walked to the kitchen. I'd carried the piece of shirt with me when I called 911, but I hadn't taken a good look at it yet. I picked it up. Black cotton. The part that I grabbed had the pocket. No one was looking, so I felt inside and found a piece of paper there. I slipped it into my pant pocket. I would take a look at it in private. If it was anything important, I could turn it over and claim to have found it later.

"She OK?" Venus said from the doorway.

"I'm fine!" Paige insisted.

"She needs to go to the hospital," the paramedic said.

"You should go, Paige," Venus said. "The last thing you need is an infection or something."

"Chanse, will you go with me?"

Paige hates hospitals. Not that anyone likes them. Her hatred of them borders on the manic. I think that something bad had happened to her in a hospital. I knew Paige better than anyone, but there were things about her that I didn't know. Most people viewed her as this smart-mouthed, strong woman who took shit from no one. It was a persona she'd affected to protect herself. But every once in a while a chink in her armor showed. Like her drinking. And pot smoking. For her, alcohol was a way to block things out. The same for her marijuana use. She rarely talked about what her life had been like before we met. It was as if she preferred me to think of her as springing into existence the night we met. "Yeah, I'll go." I turned to Venus. "You need me for anything else?"

"Is anything missing?" She looked through the piece of torn shirt.

"All major appliances are still in place." I glanced around the apartment. "All of my prints are here. My gun is still in the dresser drawer where it belongs. I don't have any jewelry and I don't keep cash in the house, and I carry my credit cards with me." The intruder wasn't there to rob me. I shivered. I remembered opening the front door, seeing the shape in the hallway. Of course, it was possible Paige and I interrupted him before he could start stealing things, but still...

"I don't think you should stay here tonight," Venus said. "You have a spare key? I'll lock up when the crime scene unit is done."

I retrieved the spare key from where I kept it in my junk drawer. I packed my gym bag with a change of clothes, toothbrush, and a few other things. I rode with Paige in the ambulance to the hospital.

The nights aren't bad in the summer. It's still humid, but without the sun beating down it's not oppressive. The hospital was OK as far as hospitals go. After Paige was admitted I walked up to the gas station on the corner to get a pack of cigarettes. I also bought a packet of rolling papers. I did have the pot in my pocket still. I found a nice big oak tree to sit behind, and rolled myself a joint. Napoleon Avenue was quiet at that time of night for a major street. A few cars went by. I just kept my head down and kept rolling. I took a drink of the Dr. Pepper that I'd bought and lit up.

I breathed in the smoke. Paige was going to be just fine. We had been lucky. I'd been lucky. Third time in four days.

This was why I don't do murders.

I don't like being shot at.

It's not fun.

It wasn't something I wanted to get used to.

I pulled the piece of paper out. Phone numbers. Seven of them. The exchanges were mostly in the French Quarter, but two were from Uptown. What were they for?

What was going on?

OK, Chanse, I said to myself, *say Mike's murder was a hate crime. Why Mike?* What was there about Mike that had made him a target? He lived in a former slave quarters apartment in one of the gayer neighborhoods of the Quarter. He would hardly have stirred up one of his neighbors. He would have been hard to miss walking down the street in a T-shirt and shorts. Would someone who didn't know him have automatically assumed he was gay? It was hard to tell. I'd only known Mike as a gay man. The guy who cuts my hair had pointed him out to me and told me he was gay. I'd seen him in gay bars. I'd seen him in a gay-owned and -operated health club. He'd been labeled "gay" in my mind from the beginning. It wasn't like he was a swishy queen. He was a muscle queen. Don't muscle queens pass for straight? Our waitress at the Bluebird had flirted with him. She hadn't seen him as gay. Paige had said that she'd thought he was gay, but Paige had a sixth sense about that kind of thing. I made a mental note to ask Paige why she had pegged him as gay.

Carrying it further, if Mike's murder was a hate crime, was it just random chance that Glen and I had been shot at? Glen was Mike's upstairs neighbor. Glen wasn't a swishy gay man, but he wasn't butch. People might not think Glen was gay. On the other hand, they might not assume he was straight either. Had Glen been the target rather than me? Maybe it was just bad luck that I was with Glen when the killer went after him. And why would the killer have been after Glen? Was it possible that Glen knew something about the murder? Maybe he'd seen the killer. Maybe he'd overheard something but hadn't realized it was important.

Maybe Glen had been the intended victim all along, rather than Mike. That was an interesting thought. But why had the wrong person been killed? And why was someone after Glen?

And how had the killer gotten into the courtyard and Mike's apartment?

Maybe the killer was someone who knew both Mike and Glen. Maybe Glen did know something.

Maybe Glen knew what these phone numbers were. I looked at my watch. Too late to call anyone now.

I went inside to wait for Paige to be released.

CHAPTER SEVENTEEN

I slept miserably on Paige's couch that night.

I've slept on her couch before. It's one of the few that I can fit on comfortably. Paige keeps her apartment at a frigid 68 degrees in the summer. That helps me fall into a deep sleep. We smoked a little pot before retiring for the night, which also helps.

What made my night's sleep miserable were the dreams. I usually don't dream. Well, that's not true; everyone dreams. I never remember mine. This night was an exception. It wasn't hard to figure out why.

The first time I woke up was from the first version of the dream. I had driven up to the front of my house. Camp Street was deserted. No one was in Coliseum Square. No cars driving by. No city bus. Nothing. No cars on the street. The streetlamp in front of my house wasn't on, and the other streetlamps were casting shadows through the trees. It was dark. Clouds hid the moon. No lights were on in any of the houses around the park. There were no signs of life. No palmetto bugs scurrying across the sidewalk. No cats prowling through the dark. It was like my entire neighborhood had been evacuated for a hurricane. Paige and I got out of the car. We didn't speak. No noise broke the stillness of the night. It was like we were afraid to break that eerie stillness. We climbed the steps to the porch. None of them made a sound. I fit the key into the front door. The door swung open, and Paige stepped inside.

There was the figure in the darkness. This time it had a face. A white face that looked as if it had never seen sunlight. It glowed in the darkness. Paige screamed.

I saw the glint of the gun.

There was the burst of light as the gun fired.

Paige screamed again and fell into me. I started screaming her name. I looked up.

The figure was gone.

I tried to get Paige to talk. She was dead.

I was covered in blood.

She felt so cold.

I woke up covered with a cold sweat. I lit a cigarette in the dark. I walked over to Paige's bedroom door. She'd taken a sleeping pill. In the dim light coming through a window I could see her calm face. Her chest was rising and settling beneath her blanket. A bit of drool was dribbling out of the side of her mouth. Reassured, I went back into the living room and sat down. I finished the cigarette and went back to sleep. Before closing my eyes I noticed that the VCR clock said 3:12.

The second dream was a variation of the first. Everything was the same. The same empty neighborhood. The same burned-out streetlamp. The same weird stillness. Only this time I was alone. I climbed the steps, every instinct in my body telling me to stop, to not go in there. Still my feet climbed the steps. Again. No groaning of wood beneath my feet. Once again the key went into the lock. Again the door swung open.

There was no one there.

I let out my breath in a sigh of relief and switched on the light.

I screamed.

Paul was lying naked on the floor. Blood was everywhere. And on the wall, I saw it. Those horrible words. Written in blood. Little trails of blood snaking down the wall from the writing.

FAGGOTS DIE.

I screamed and screamed and screamed.

And sat up on the couch.

4:48, according to the VCR.

I reached for another cigarette. My hand was shaking. *Just a dream,* I told myself. *It was just a dream. It's no wonder you're having nightmares. Who wouldn't after everything that's been going down over the last couple of days?* I started a pot of coffee. I wished that Paige was awake. I checked in on her while the coffee was brewing. She hadn't even shifted. The only thing different was how much drool was on her face. I brushed my teeth, shivering because the apartment was so damned cold.

My stomach was growling, so I rooted through the refrigerator. The only things inside were some snacks, a half-gallon of skim milk, a 12-pack of diet Coke, and two Styrofoam take-out containers. Paige was not big on cooking. She was proud of the fact she couldn't scramble an egg. She liked eating out and had a menu for every eatery in Uptown that delivered.

I opened the first container and almost gagged. The half-eaten chicken nachos had fuzzy green spots of mold dotting the cheese. I quickly put the container back and opened the other. Cold French fries and part of a mushroom cheeseburger. I chewed on the cold fries and waited for the coffee to finish brewing. I put the cheeseburger in the microwave. She wouldn't care if I ate it. Paige saves half-finished meals for weeks. She claims to hate wasting food, but it always ends up going into the trash anyway.

The cheeseburger wasn't bad. The coffee sort of warmed me up. I pulled on my shorts and shirt, wishing I'd thought to bring sweats. I wrapped myself up in my blanket and turned on the television. I watched auto racing for an hour or two on ESPN. Talk about excitement. There was something Zen-like in watching the cars going around and around while I drank my coffee.

I just wanted to forget everything for a while. Oddly enough, watching auto racing did the trick for me. By the time the sun came up and auto racing gave way to kids on Rollerblades doing tricks that looked dangerous, I felt better. I turned off the coffeepot and wrote Paige a quick note. I was going out to get a few things and check the damage to my apartment.

I hit the Burger King drive-through to get something to eat, then bypassed the yellow crime-scene tape and opened my front door. My apartment was a wreck. A thin layer of fingerprint powder covered the entire place, and there were black footprints all over the hardwood floors. That was going to be fun to clean up.

There were no messages on the answering machine. I had hoped there would be a message from Paul. It would be comforting to hear his voice, even on a recording. I looked around at the mess. I hated seeing my apartment like this. I'm not a clean freak by any stretch, but I like my place to be cleaner than this. This was too much. Christ.

I walked into the bedroom and packed a suitcase. The lock on the outside door to my bedroom was broken. I walked over to it. That was how he'd gotten in. It couldn't have been hard. The locks on the doors would only stop the laziest of crooks. I never used my security system. I'd forgotten the code. I made a mental note to call the property manager and get the code again. I lugged my suitcase back to the car, locked up, and headed back to Paige's.

Paige was reading the paper when I got back. "Isn't Glen Chandler the upstairs neighbor? Mike's, I mean?"

"Yeah. Why?"

Grimly, she handed the paper to me. On page 4 there was a small notice. The headline screamed "Gay Bashing in French Quarter." I scanned it quickly and felt my stomach turn sour. Apparently, Glen had been walking home from a trip to La Madeleine on Jackson Square when he was jumped and beaten on Dumaine Street. He'd been punched and kicked. His attackers had called him things like "faggot," "cocksucker," and "sodomite." I ran my hands through my hair. "What the hell is happening?" I asked.

"It's getting ugly." Paige lit a cigarette. "I'm telling you, Chanse, they'd better find Mike's killer and fast. It won't be long before this violence escalates."

"What do you mean?"

"Come on," she said. "How long do you think it's going to be before someone like Jarrett Phillips starts inciting the queer community to retaliate? It's the next step."

"The candlelight vigil?"

"Don't you think that's the logical place for something bad to happen?"

I stared at her.

"Something's wrong with this whole thing, Chanse. You know it, I know it, Venus knows it. Mike's murder wasn't a hate crime. Jarrett Phillips and his organization have jumped on the bandwagon, advancing their political agenda, and they're stirring up a lot of emotion and tension in town." She flicked an ash into an ashtray, missing by several inches. "You and Glen were shot at the other night. That didn't make it into the newspaper or onto the local news. What happened last night didn't either, because I called in some favors. But Glen was gay-bashed, and there it is in the paper. And I'm betting that it was on the 10 o'clock news last night. All the homophobes in town who've kept their mouths shut are starting to come out of the wood-work. Jarrett is trying to stir up the queer community." She put out her cigarette. "I'm not saying this wasn't a golden opportunity for him—a murder that looks like an antigay hate crime. But there's still a sodomy law on the books here in Louisiana, and I'm telling you, if it came down to a vote, the good people of Louisiana would keep it on the books. Overwhelmingly. Jarrett's getting a lot of press cov-erage, and he's stirring up a lot of repressed hatred and homophobia amongst all the good ol' boys and right-wing Christians. Do you really think this vigil tonight is going to come off peacefully?"

I didn't say anything for a minute. "You know, maybe Glen was the target the other night when we were shot at."

"It's kind of a coincidence that he was shot at one night and beaten up the next, isn't it?"

"But someone broke in last night and tried to kill me too." The thought made me nauseous. "So it's possible it was me they were shooting at the other night."

"And just a coincidence that Glen got beaten up?"

"How did whoever it was know that I'd be on Dauphine at just that time?" I said.

And then I remembered something. Glen and I were sitting in Kaldi's. He'd just invited me to his place. But before we left, he'd said, "I just have to make a phone call before we go." Which he did. I said to Paige, "Glen made a phone call before we left Kaldi's."

Paige handed me one of her cigarettes. I lit it and inhaled. She lit one for herself as well. "Do you think Glen might have tipped someone off about where you'd be?"

"It's a possibility." I took another drag. I hated her cigarettes. They tasted like dog shit rolled in paper. "Maybe it was the same people who beat him up last night. Maybe he made them mad for whatever reason, and they decided to teach him a lesson."

"You think he's in on it with the homophobes?"

"No." I shook my head. "I don't think any of this has to do with homophobia. I really don't. Someone is trying very hard to make all of this look like a series of hate crimes. But it's not. It's something else."

"The only person gaining from this is Jarrett Phillips," Paige said.

"Paige, I'm willing to believe that Jarrett is blackmailing closet cases to fund his organization. But I can't believe that he's killing people and having people beaten up."

"Is murder such a far step from blackmail? Once you start breaking the law, what's one more crime?"

She had a point. Once you've forged a check, why stop there? Why not use someone's credit card? Then why not steal someone's credit card? And on and on. Like dominoes.

It was the same argument the antidrug crusaders made about smoking pot. Once you've smoked pot, you'll move on to cocaine. Then heroin. And once you've done heroin, anything goes. "Maybe I should call Glen to make sure he's OK."

"Maybe you should." Paige's eyes narrowed. "See how accurate this coverage is."

I got out my wallet and pulled out the card with his number on it. It rang five times, and the machine picked up. "Hey, this is Glen. I'm not here obviously, so leave a message and I might call you back if you're lucky." *Beep.*

"Hey, Glen, this is Chanse, I just wanted to call and make sure—"

"Chanse?" Glen sounded a little breathless when he picked up the phone. "I'm screening calls."

"Are you OK?"

"I guess." He laughed. "You should see my face. I called in sick at the airport—no point in scaring passengers. I have a fat lip, a black eye, cuts and scrapes all over. My body is a great big bruise."

"What happened?"

"I went down to La Madeleine for some French bread. I wanted to make pasta for dinner, and I thought some garlic bread would be nice. No big deal, right? So I'm walking back up St. Ann, and everything's cool, you know? Waved at some friends at the Pub when I went by there, stopped and chatted for a bit—no big deal, typical early evening in the Quarter, you know? Then I walked up to Dauphine and started toward home. When I got about halfway up the block this car pulls up. Three guys jump out, call me names, and start pounding on me."

"Jesus."

"When they knocked me out, I guess they thought they'd killed me or something, 'cause the last thing I remember is falling to the sidewalk and getting kicked, and then I woke up in a lot of pain, and no one was around."

"Didn't anybody see it happen?"

"No one claims to." He made a noise. "Right up the street from all the gay bars. I mean, for God's sake, Good Friends is right there on the corner! And no one saw anything?" He uttered a half sob. "I'm putting in a transfer. I'm not staying here anymore. It's too dangerous to be gay here. Next time they might kill me."

"Do you need anything?" My mind was racing.

"No. Can I call you later, though?"

"Sure." I hung up without giving him Paige's number. The last thing he needed to hear was that someone had broken into my apartment and shot Paige. I sat on the couch next to her. "How are you feeling?"

She shrugged. "It's a little sore, but not bad."

I pulled the list of phone numbers out of my pocket. I handed it to her. "I found this last night. It was in the guy's pocket."

"Phone numbers," She said. "French Quarter exchanges." She tossed me the cordless phone. "Call one."

"I should probably turn this over to Venus."

"You don't know the attacker dropped it." Paige winked at me slowly. "You just happened to find it after he left. Anyone could have dropped this in your apartment."

"Yeah." But I wasn't 100% sure Venus would buy that argument. Especially if the list turned out to be evidence.

"Why don't you give the first number a call and see who it is?"

I turned the phone on. I dialed the number and waited. After two rings, a recorded message picked up. "Please enter your phone number followed by the pound key." I did. I put the phone down. "It's a pager."

"Guess we'll find out who it is when they call back," Paige said. "Not much else to do. I wonder if they're all pagers?"

The phone rang, and I answered. "Hello?"

"Someone paged me from this number?" It was a man's voice. He sounded young. Early 20s, maybe.

"Well, yes."

"Well, I don't have any free time this evening. It's kind of late to be calling for tonight anyway." He sounded impatient. "I'm with a client right now. Can I call you back when he leaves?"

"What are your rates?"

"$200 per hour for an out call."

"That's a little high, isn't it?"

"I'm worth it. Do you want me to call you back or not?"

"Never mind."

He gave an exasperated sigh and hung up. I turned the phone off and set it down on the coffee table. "An escort," I said.

"So I gathered." She leaned back in her chair. "You think they're all escorts?"

"Let's find out."

One by one we called the numbers. In each case, the call back was from an escort.

"Dial the next one and make an appointment for tomorrow," Paige said.

"I'm not going to pay—"

"I'll pay for it and expense it to the paper." She sipped

her wine. "I wonder why our gunman was carrying around a list of escorts' pager numbers?"

"Maybe he prefers to pay for sex." An older friend of mine was like that. He wanted no romantic entanglements whatsoever. Whenever he felt horny, he ordered an escort. He insisted it was more honest than picking someone up in a bar. In a bar everyone is operating under the illusion that they are all looking for a relationship when all they want is sex. Inevitably, feelings get hurt. And there's always the chance the person could turn out to be crazy or a stalker. So if you just want to get laid, call an escort and spend some cash. The escort is only in it for the money. You won't have to see him again unless you get horny again. No emotions. No entanglements. You're in complete control when you pay for it.

I picked up the phone and dialed the next number. I listened to the instructions, followed them, and hung up the phone. This time the phone rang immediately.

"Hello?"

"Someone paged me?" This voice was a little higher-pitched than the last one.

"Yes, I was wondering if I could make an appointment with you for tomorrow afternoon?"

"An out call?"

"Yes."

"Out calls are $250 per hour. How long you gonna want?"

"Um, an hour should be fine."

"What do you want? Top or bottom? Any fantasy role-play? That costs more."

"No fantasy. I just want a nice fuck."

Paige was shaking with laughter.

"You have to wear a condom. You want me to bring them?"

"Sure."

"Address?" I gave him the address and directions. We set a time for 2 o'clock the next afternoon. He hung up.

"You 'just want a nice fuck.'" Paige giggled some more.

"I don't know what to say to these guys. It's not like I've hired one before."

"Well, you're not going to get to fuck this one," Paige said. "A list of escorts' phone numbers: What's the connection?"

"Maybe there isn't one." I picked up the phone and dialed the last number on the list. Might as well make sure they were all escorts. After leaving my numeric message I hung up. Several minutes passed before the phone rang. I answered. "Hello?"

"Someone paged me?"

I froze.

"Hello? Hello?"

I disconnected the call and put the phone down slowly. Paige was staring at me. "What's wrong, Chanse?"

"That was Glen Chandler."

"The neighbor? The one who was just gay-bashed?"

I nodded. "One and the same."

"You up to the vigil tonight?" When I nodded, she smiled. "Wouldn't miss a chance to see Jarrett in all of his glory, would you?"

CHAPTER EIGHTEEN

Paige and I found it interesting that the candlelight vigil was going to be held in the mall between Jackson Square and St. Louis Cathedral. Gay events are usually held in Washington Square in the Marigny. While there is a large gay presence in the Quarter, it's larger in the Marigny. On the other hand, Jackson Square is better known than Washington Square. And Jackson Square is beautifully landscaped. The equestrian statue of President Andrew Jackson is a popular place for tourists to have their pictures taken. Jackson Square, for a lot of people, *is* New Orleans.

"He probably wants to be on television with the cathedral behind him," Paige said as I parked the car on Ursulines Street. "Much more dramatic than the houses on Frenchmen Street."

She was probably right.

Paige tucked her arm through mine. We were both a little nervous, given that I'd been shot at twice and Paige had been shot at once — and hit. Not to mention Mike's death and Glen's being beaten senseless. I didn't know if these were hate crimes, but the possibility nagged at me. Maybe to a homophobic stranger we'd look like any other straight couple.

Yeah, right.

We walked up Ursulines and turned right onto Bourbon. I didn't feel like walking up Dauphine. Bourbon was more populated than Dauphine. The more people, the safer it was. We walked in silence.

When we reached Dumaine, Paige said, "It's still early. Let's grab a beer." She ducked into Cafe Lafitte in Exile. Frowning, I followed her in.

"I see you've got your candles," Jamie Kelso said from behind the bar as Paige ordered two drafts. "We're giving them away for free." Jamie had been bartending the afternoon/early-evening shift at Lafitte's for as long as I could remember. He would be attractive if he lost some weight. He had blue-black hair, bright blue eyes, and the longest eyelashes I've ever seen on a man not wearing drag. Jamie rented out a couple of double-shotgun houses he owned in the Irish Channel. Between that and his tips he made a decent living. Better than mine anyway. He set down two to-go cups in front of us.

Paige looked at me. I paid him, leaving a couple of bucks on the bar as a tip. "Think there'll be a big turnout?"

Jamie rolled his eyes. "It's all anyone is talking about."

"What are the heteros saying?" Paige sipped her beer. I wasn't sure if she was supposed to have alcohol with her pain medication. *This could get interesting,* I thought.

"A lot of straight people are going to be there," Jamie said. "I mean, everyone in the Quarter is sick of crime, period. Oh, check this out." He reached down behind the counter and handed us a flyer.

I looked at it. It was hot pink. There was an attractive picture of Mike Hansen from the torso up in the center of it. He was shirtless and smiling for the camera. He looked about as innocent and fresh as a daisy. He didn't look like the opportunistic whore that everyone seemed to think he was. Over the picture was a header in screaming black letters:

MIKE HANSEN COULD HAVE BEEN ANY ONE OF US!

Underneath, the flyer read:

A political funeral for Mike Hansen will be held in front of St. Louis Cathedral Thursday at 8 P.M. Light a candle as gays, lesbians, transgendered persons, and bisexuals take back the night.
WE WILL NOT BE AFRAID ANYMORE.

"Political funeral?" I looked at Paige. "I thought it was a vigil. What the hell is a political funeral?"

"They're very common in Latin America." Paige lit a cigarette. "In repressive regimes, when a political prisoner is executed, the opposition holds these huge rallies. They call them political funerals. It's a way of letting the government know that the victim was not alone."

"I don't like the sound of this," I said slowly.

"The bars are closing for two hours during the funeral," Jamie said with a grimace.

"The bars are closing?" I looked at Paige in amazement. The Quarter bars stayed open during hurricanes. I'd never known any of the bars to close, ever.

Jamie nodded. "In support for Mike Hansen." He laughed. "That fucking whore. I keep thinking that I'm going to wake up and find out this whole thing is some weird dream."

"Did you know Mike?" Paige asked. She was almost finished with her beer.

Jamie nodded. "Honey, every bartender in the Quarter knew her. She was one of the biggest tramps in the city. She had two requirements to get naked—a great body or a big bank account." He shook his head. "All this fuss over a piece of bar trash. Go figure."

"Come on, Chanse, let's go." Paige headed for the door out onto Bourbon Street. As we walked up toward St. Ann, several houses were flying the rainbow flags. Some had posters hanging from the balconies:

GAYS—VICTIMS NO MORE

NO MORE HATE CRIMES

NEW ORLEANS SAFE FOR EVERYONE

NO MORE POLICE HARASSMENT

"Chanse, this is scary," Paige said.

I nodded. There was a huge banner hanging across Bourbon Street from the Parade's balcony over to Oz's.

GAYS TAKE BACK THE NIGHT

NO MORE HATE CRIMES OR POLICE HARASSMENT

"I don't like this at all," I said.

"The Quarter is a powder keg," Paige whispered. "Just waiting for someone to light the fuse."

"I don't think it's going to come to that." We walked in front of the doors to the Pub. A couple of men I had never seen before were standing there drinking. One spat at the ground in front of us. "Fucking straight people," he said.

I stopped. "What did you say?"

"You heard me, breeder."

"Come on, Chanse." Paige tugged at my arm. I stood there for a minute, staring at his drunken face. He hadn't shaved in several days. He was wearing a black T-shirt with a large pink triangle on it, and a pair of dirty white jeans shorts. I started to walk away when he threw his drink at me. The wet, cold liquid drenched my head and dripped onto my neck. I grabbed him by the throat. "You son of a bitch!" I pulled my fist back and was going to let it fly. The Pub's security guard jumped in between us.

"No, Chanse! No!" The Pub's security guard was a bodybuilder named Billy Boucree. I had seen him around Bodytech a few times. He was a nice guy.

I let go of the jerk's neck.

"Fucking breeder!" The jerk spit in my face.

Before I could do anything, Billy punched him in the face three times. The drunk fell back against the wall and slumped to the ground.

"You don't pull that shit in my bar, asshole," Billy snarled. "And for your information, asshole, Chanse is one of us."

One of us.

Billy handed me a bar towel. I wiped the spit off my face and mopped the drink out of my hair. I was shaking, I was so angry.

One of us.

I handed Billy the towel and took Paige's arm and walked up St. Ann toward Jackson Square.

One of us.

It had come to that.

Us vs. them.

Gays vs. straights.

"Maybe we should just go home," Paige said, stopping to light a cigarette at the corner of Royal. "I have a bad feeling about this."

Just as she said that, about five mounted police officers rode by on their horses in the direction of the Square. We looked at each other. We could already hear the noise. It sounded like a huge crowd was gathering. It was sort of like Mardi Gras, only there was no laughter. It was more like a low buzz, lots of murmuring. We could see people crossing St. Ann a block further up, all carrying candles, some carrying rainbow flags. Some were wearing hot-pink T-shirts. Some were carrying signs. All of them had grim expressions on their faces. Paige shrugged and threw her cigarette into the street. "Well, I am a reporter, after all." We walked up St. Ann.

Jackson Square was packed with people. Everywhere. Even the pedestrian malls on either side of the iron fence around the park. A speaker's stand was set up at the foot of the cathedral steps. There were camera crews everywhere. All the local news stations were represented. There were police officers everywhere too, some on horses, some on foot. We stood in front of La Madeleine, at the corner of St. Ann and Chartres, and looked around. I recognized more people than I thought I would. All segments of the gay community were represented—club kids, drag queens, leathermen in full regalia, muscle queens, preppies. It looked like Gay Pride without the festive air.

Paige shivered. I put my arm around her. There were dark clouds in the sky. The air was thick and heavy. My hair, damp from the drink, was getting drenched with sweat. It was hot. Crowds gathering in this kind of heat were not a good thing.

Jarrett Phillips climbed onto the speaker's stand and stepped up to the microphone. "Here we go," Paige muttered. "Let the games begin."

An ear-splitting burst of feedback blasted through the sound system. Jarrett stepped back from the microphone for a moment with a smile. "Thank you for coming, brothers and sisters."

A roar of cheers and applause rose from the crowd. Paige squeezed my hand.

"We are gathered here today for what we have termed a political funeral," Jarrett proclaimed. "Mike Hansen was murdered just a few short days ago in what we can only consider to be a political crime. He was murdered, shot to death in his apartment for no other reason than that he had the nerve in this day and age to live his life as an openly gay man. That was his only crime, because that was what his murderers considered his sexuality and lifestyle to be— a crime. His killers were sending a message to all of us— get back into the closet; any lifestyle that doesn't fit in with our Judeo-Christian value system will be stamped out! By violence, if need be!

"It is doubly ironic that we are holding this rally in front of one of the oldest symbols in this country of the unforgiving religion that has spilled more blood in its name than any other religion in recorded history. The Christian Church is the enemy! The hatred that the Christian leaders preach is what has led to this crime. A church that is supposedly founded upon principles of love and peace is actually nothing more than a bloodthirsty oppressor, making

Adolf Hitler look like a child! Well, I say, *no more*!" The last words were shouted, thundering and echoing off the Pontalba buildings. The crowd let out an even louder roar of approval. "Now, let us light our candles in a moment of silence for Mike Hansen and every other victim of the Fascist Christian religion." All over the park, matches and lighters flared as candles were lit. Paige and I lit ours.

"Faggots," an older woman hissed as she walked past us.

"The wages of *sin* are death and eternal damnation!" an amplified voice roared, breaking the silence. I looked up. On the other side of the church, on St. Peter Street, a huge truck had pulled up. It was surrounded by people carrying picket signs: AIDS CURES FAGS, HOMOS BURN IN HELL, and other equally pithy slogans. The back of the truck had a huge cross mounted on it. A man standing on the roof of the cab shouted into a bullhorn, "Repent! Give up your sinful lives!"

"Oh, God," Paige lit a cigarette from her candle flame. The camera crews set up in front of Jarrett's stage swung around and began filming the Christian counterdemonstration.

"There is the enemy!" Jarrett screamed into his microphone. The gay crowd began to mutter and murmur amongst themselves. "They are the ones who want to put you back into the closet and slam the door!"

"*God* is the way to salvation!" the man standing on the cab bawled.

"*Damn your God!*" Jarrett boomed. One of the Christian demonstrators moved to the edge of the gay crowd and started shouting at a lesbian in leather.

"Chanse! Up on the roof!"

I looked over to where Paige was pointing. Up on the roof of the Pontalba was a man with a rifle. "Oh, my God," I said. I started moving toward one of the mounted policemen. I saw a flash of light from the rifle. The retort of the gunshot echoed loudly throughout the park. Jarrett clutched his chest and fell backward off the stage. For a moment, there was stunned silence. Then it turned ugly. Someone screamed, and people started running as another gunshot ricocheted off the front of the cathedral. I grabbed Paige by the arm and started pulling her down Chartres Street. Behind us we heard pandemonium.

We ran all the way back to the car. I started it and headed for the highway. I wanted to get as far away from the Quarter as I could. My heart was pounding. Paige was breathing hard. I'd never seen a riot before. When I turned onto the on ramp for I-10, there was a flash of lightning and a roar of thunder.

The skies opened.

We drove back to Paige's in silence.

CHAPTER NINETEEN

As soon as we got back to Paige's apartment, she switched on her computer and started typing. I knew she was writing a piece on what had just happened in Jackson Square. I might as well be a piece of furniture until she was finished. I ordered us a large thick-crust pizza with extra cheese, pepperoni, mushroom, onion, and jalapeño, and then I poured her a glass of red wine. She nodded when I set it on her desk. Her fingers were flying across the keyboard; her brow knit was together, her eyes narrowed. I loaded my pipe and turned on the television. The riot in Jackson Square was bound to be the lead news story on all of the local networks. I was curious to see what their take on the incident would be. I took a hit from the pipe and flipped through the channels. I wondered if Jarrett was dead. I didn't like him, but I didn't want him dead—especially if a sniper atop the Pontalba had provided the fatal bullet. Maybe we'd been cowards, fleeing the way we had. Maybe we should have stayed and seen if we could have helped anyone who may have been hurt.

Or been shot or hurt ourselves.

Maybe leaving was the smart thing to do. I don't consider myself a coward. But there's nothing brave about confronting someone with a gun unless there's no other option. I don't think I'm that tough. I know I'm not tough enough to withstand a bullet wound. Lead won't bounce off my skin. Hey, I'm not Superman.

Sue me.

I flipped by something that looked like Jackson Square, so I went back. Sure enough, it was Jackson Square on CNN. It was raining. The square was completely deserted. The reporter was standing underneath one of the Pontalba awnings.

"Behind me you see fabled Jackson Square, one of the more famous landmarks in New Orleans. Jackson Square is peaceful and quiet now, but just over an hour ago it was anything but." The segment cut to a shot of the crowd holding candles during the moment of silence as the reporter continued in voiceover, "What local gay activists were calling a political funeral was disrupted, first by a group of Christian counterdemonstrators and then by something even more sinister." Cut to a picture of Mike Hansen. He was standing in front of Oz, wearing tight jean shorts, no shirt, and a big smile. "Four days ago, Michael Hansen was found shot to death in his apartment in the French Quarter. Written in his blood on one of the walls were the words 'faggots die.'" Cut to an extremely uncomfortable-looking Ronnie Bishop. "Hansen's former lover, Ronnie Bishop, was horrified by the shooting." Cut to a close-up of Ronnie's face.

"Mike was a sweet guy, Everyone liked him. It's hard to believe that anyone would kill him just because he was gay. He never hurt anyone." Ronnie said.

The segment cut back to the reporter. I stared at the television in disbelief. I had not heard Ronnie Bishop say on national television that everyone liked Mike, had I? The reporter went on, "The murder has the gay community of New Orleans reeling."

An image of Jarrett Phillips in his office flashed onto the screen. "Unfortunately, the killing does not surprise Jarrett Phillips, executive director of Gay Rights Now!, an activist nonprofit organization in the Big Easy," the reporter stated.

"Everyone thinks New Orleans is this liberal city where anything goes," Jarrett was saying, an earnest look on his face. "You know, let the good times roll and all of that. It's not that way at all. New Orleans is an extremely conservative city—underneath all the Carnival trappings and free-flowing alcohol. There are hundreds of gay bashings a year that the police never bother to investigate. Yet they can find time to raid gay bars and arrest people for what they call 'lewd conduct,' a broad term that covers everything from urinating in public to soliciting for prostitution to two men kissing on the street. They entrap runaways who live on the streets and have to sell their bodies for food, and they cart them off to the state penitentiary in Angola. But investigate a gay bashing? They don't have time for that. The detective in charge of the investigation into this murder has publicly stated that she does not consider this a hate crime, despite the ugly words scrawled on the wall in the victim's blood."

Back to the reporter in Jackson Square. "Phillips organized tonight's political funeral for our country's latest hate- crime victim. But what started as a peaceful rally to show the solidarity of the New Orleans gay community soon turned into something no one could have foreseen."

The camera cut to a tape of the rally. The truck with the Christians rolled into view, their placards plainly visible.

"The rally was disrupted by members of the Church of Our Savior, a far-right fundamentalist denomination that is very antigay." Cut to the confrontation between the sign wielder and the lesbian in leather—and then something I hadn't seen. The sign wielder spat on the lesbian, who punched her. One of the male Christians then went after the lesbian, who kneed him viciously in the crotch. Other gays and lesbians ran over and joined in, and a large fistfight broke out. "And then a sniper opened fire." The rifle shot echoed as the report cut to a great shot of Jarrett falling backward off the stage. Then there were screams and a mass of people fleeing the scene. The reporter came back into view. "Phillips was not hurt by the sniper's bullet other than a cracked rib. On the advice of his security team, he was wearing a bulletproof vest. But 37 people were hospitalized in the pandemonium that broke out after the sniper began firing.

"There is currently a new ordinance in front of the City Council of New Orleans to add gays and lesbians to the groups covered under the city's current hate-crime legisla-tion. Many gays and lesbians will not rest easy in the Big Easy until it is passed."

I turned the television off. Jarrett had to be pleased. He'd been on CNN. I took another hit.

"Thirty-seven people," Paige said as she pushed her chair back from her desk and stretched. "I wonder what would've happened if that sniper hadn't shown up when he did?"

"Huh?"

She lit a cigarette. "It was getting ugly, Chanse. You saw the tape. It was turning into a riot. The gunshots stopped it."

"You're telling me the gunman's purpose wasn't to kill Jarrett but to stop a riot from happening?" I shook my head.

"Sorry, darlin', not even Oliver Stone would buy into that theory."

She shrugged. "Kind of interesting that he happened to be wearing a bulletproof vest, don't you think?" She jumped as the doorbell rang. "Who the hell is that?"

"The pizza boy." I opened the door. The poor guy was drenched. I paid him. It smelled wonderful. I was starving. Paige got plates. We helped ourselves to gooey slices, dripping with melted cheese and grease.

"Yum." Paige wiped some grease off her chin with a paper towel. "Thanks for ordering this. I'm starved."

"No problem."

"Let me ask you this." She chewed for a moment. "Have you changed your mind about the hate-crime aspect of Mike's murder after all of this?"

I sat back and thought for a minute. "It's possible that all of the violence of the last couple of days was triggered by Mike's murder but otherwise unrelated to it. I mean, Mike's killer made it look like a hate crime. And the appearance of a hate crime could have set the ball in motion for the rest of the violence. But that's the problem—what's related to the actual killing and what isn't? I think Glen and I being shot at was related to the killing. I think the intruder in my apartment was related to the killing. That can't be a coincidence. The sniper in the square could be unrelated."

"What about Glen's mugging? You think that was independent as well?"

"That's hard. I mean, it's possible that he just happened to be in the wrong place at the wrong time. But twice? And both times right after his neighbor is killed? That's too many coincidences—and let's not forget that Glen's pager number was on the burglar who tried to kill us." I shuddered at the thought.

"Maybe Mr. Glen knows a little bit more about the murder than he's letting on." Paige leaned back with a sigh. She'd eaten three pieces of pizza quickly. She lit a cigarette.

I finished my fourth slice and closed the box. I was full. I lit a cigarette myself. "I've been wondering about that. I mean, I wasn't involved in this thing the night we were shot at. Maybe Glen was the target instead of me."

"It's possible." Paige got up and walked over to her computer. She started typing as she talked. "It can't just be a coincidence that his pager number was on the burglar. Ah, here we go." Her printer started spitting out something. "I love E-mail." She picked up the paper and handed it to me. "Here are your doctors who were King of Rex."

There were three names on the printout. Three doctors had been King of Rex in the last 15 years. One was dead, another was in his late 60s, and the third...I whistled. "Bryce Dubuisson," I said out loud.

Dr. Bryce Dubuisson. Doctor to the privileged. From one of the oldest, snobbiest, wealthiest families in New Orleans. Married with three teenage children. A big mansion in the Garden District on the corner of Third Street and Coliseum. A fortune in the tens of millions.

I had met him at one of my landlady's interminable parties. The purpose of this invitation was to set me up with the son of one of her closest Garden District buddies. This guy was fresh out of Stanford Law and determined to dedicate his career to gay legal causes. In San Francisco. His mother wanted him to join an old and respected firm here. He was good-looking enough, had a nice body, but all he wanted to talk about was the injustices that gays face in today's world. I walked away after a few minutes of listening to him preach and sat on a deck chair by the pool.

"Mind if I join you?"

"Nah," I replied without looking up. Barbara's parties aren't much fun for me. All that drinking, gossip, and food. It was all about who got the drunkest and made the biggest ass of himself. People would talk about it for weeks, or at least until the next party.

"My name is Bryce Dubuisson." He held out his hand. I shook it. He was a handsome man in his early 40s. His hair was graying and cut short. His grip was strong, his palm dry. He was wearing a pair of white cotton slacks, a white button-down shirt that had probably cost $200, and a pair of penny loafers with no socks. He wasn't wearing an undershirt—major faux pas in that crowd. His nipples were evident against the cotton of his shirt. In the fading light, I couldn't tell what color his eyes were. They looked warm and friendly. He was clean-shaven with olive-colored skin, a strong nose, and a dimple in his chin.

"Chanse MacLeod," I replied. We sat in silence for a few moments. I got the distinct impression on several occasions that he was going to say something, but he never did. After about five minutes his wife came looking for him— one of those Southern ladies with the high-pitched voice who drinks too much. He left with her on his arm. My gaydar hadn't gone off. Maybe it had short-circuited from prolonged contact with the activist. I was impressed when Bryce was named King of Rex the following year.

"Dr. Dubuisson?" Paige frowned.

"He's the logical choice," I said. If he was gay, he wouldn't want anyone to know. His father, Antoine Dubuisson, was pretty old. Lots of money. Lots of social standing. It fit. "Guess I'll have to have a chat with Dr. Bryce." I looked at the clock on the wall. "It'll have to wait until tomorrow, though. Too late to call him now."

Paige nodded. "Yeah." She yawned. "You staying over again?"

I nodded. "I'll get up early to catch him at his office."

I set the alarm and stared at the ceiling. I heard Paige rummaging around in her room.

Escorts.

Closeted society doctors.

Christ.

CHAPTER TWENTY

I got up early the next morning. I didn't wake Paige. I didn't see any point in it. She was snoring. If you wake her too early she's a total bitch for the rest of the day. I left a note on the coffeemaker and slipped out.

It was a beautiful morning. No clouds in the sky. The sky was a vibrant deep blue. It was still hot. The humidity had not broken with the storm. The pavement seemed to be steaming. I turned on the air-conditioning and drove down Napoleon Avenue. Napoleon is one of my favorite streets in the city. I love the big old oak trees that line it, the beautiful houses on either side, and the smell of flowers. Napoleon is just as beautiful as St. Charles.

Bryce Dubuisson's office was in a medical building on Prytania Street near Touro Hospital. I pulled into the parking lot. The front doors were open. I found his office number on the directory and walked into the lobby. A nurse behind a sliding glass partition smiled at me. "Can I help you?"

"Is Dr. Dubuisson in yet?"

"No, but I expect him at any moment."

It would be better to corner him in the parking lot, I decided. "Thanks." I smiled and walked out.

I wanted coffee but was afraid to leave. I didn't want to miss him. I sat outside and smoked a cigarette. Maybe 10 minutes passed before a silver Lexus drove in and parked. It was him.

He looked a little older than he had when I'd met him at Barbara's party—a little grayer, a little more lined, but still in good shape. I waited for him to lock his car and then approached.

"Dr. Dubuisson?"

He looked at me, startled. Recognition dawned on his face as he tried to place my face. "Yes?"

"We met a couple of years ago at a party at Barbara Castlemaine's," I offered helpfully.

"Yes, that's it." He smiled and shook my hand. Firm grip. He was a handsome man. "You're Chase? Charles? Something like that."

"Chanse MacLeod." I let go of his hand. "Do you have a moment? I'd like to ask you a few questions."

"Quick ones." He glanced at his watch. "I just have a few minutes."

"Did you know Mike Hansen?"

He hesitated for a moment. It was just a slight pause, but it was enough to convince me. "No, I can't say that I did."

Well, I hadn't expected him to admit it.

"Then you aren't being blackmailed?"

"I don't have time for this nonsense." He walked past me.

"I can't help you, if you don't help me." I followed him to the door.

"I don't need any help." He walked in without a backward glance.

It was him, all right. I shook my head. But how could I get him to admit to it? It had been worth a shot, though. I got back in my car and drove home.

The crime-scene tape around my front door had been removed. I'm sure that pleased my next-door neighbor. I parked on the street. I unlocked the front door and stepped into an even worse disaster than when I'd been there to pack a suitcase. I'd left the ceiling fans on, and they had scattered fingerprint dust everywhere. Several days worth of mail had accumulated on the floor under the drop slot. I picked it up: Junk, junk, junk, more junk, still more junk. At least no bills. I tossed the stack into the garbage. I looked at the answering machine. Four messages. I hit play and got the broom out of the closet.

Beep. "Hey, Chanse, where are you? This is Paul calling from Albuquerque. Having a nice visit with my folks and my brothers. You'll have to come out here with me some- time. I've told my family about you, and they want to meet you. I'll try again later, OK? I love you."

There it was again—those three little words that had always sent me running. I started sweeping the floor. Now he'd said it twice. Granted, only to the machine. But he wanted me to meet his family. What was going on? Appar- ently we'd crossed into another stage of our relationship. It would've been nice if someone had bothered to tell me. I liked Paul, I enjoyed his company, he had a great body, and the sex was out of this world. But was I in love with him?

Beep. "Chanse, it's Glen. I wanted to call and say thanks for your concern. It's Thursday afternoon, and I was hop- ing maybe you could come by for dinner tonight. I was curious if you were going to the rally tonight. Call me, OK?"

Ah, Glen. I found it ironic that the one person since meeting Paul that I'd been attracted to turned out to be a male whore. I supposed that he had his reasons for doing it. It still bugged me, though. He was a nice-looking guy with a great personality. He was obviously smart. Was it necessary for him to make extra cash by prostitution? I mean, sure, the money had to be great. I wish I could charge my clients $200 per hour. But wasn't it demeaning? And I'd always pictured whores as drug-addicted losers forced to sell their bodies because they had no other way of making money. OK, so some strippers supplement their incomes from dancing by hustling. They couldn't all be drug addicts, not with the bodies they display in their G-strings while performing in the bars. Porn stars hustle too, but porn stars were whores simply by being porn stars. They had sex on videotape for money. It wasn't a big stretch for them to be hustling. But Glen? Smart, funny, cute Glen? Cute, funny, smart Glen, who said that Mike hadn't considered him good enough to sleep with?

Glen, a whore?

It didn't add up.

Beep. "Chanse, this is Jarrett Phillips. I'm hoping that you'll show up for the political funeral we're holding for Mike in Jackson Square this evening. I know that you persist in believing this wasn't a political crime against the gay community, but you should show up this evening."

Fuck off.

Beep. "Chanse, this is Remy Deveraux. It's Thursday evening, about 9 o'clock. I was wondering if you could call me here at the house tonight, or failing that, at my office tomorrow morning?" He left both numbers.

I stopped sweeping. What could that be about? I picked up the phone and called Remy's office. He must have left instructions to put me right through. "Remy? Chanse MacLeod. What's up?"

"Chanse! Thank God that you called." Remy spoke very softly. "I found out something yesterday afternoon that might interest to you."

"What's that?"

"I don't want to talk about it over the phone. Can you meet me for lunch?"

I looked at the clock on my wall. It was 10. I had to be back at Paige's to meet our hustler at 2 o'clock. "If it's an early lunch."

"Well, hell." Remy took a deep breath. "I'll just tell you now. Why should I be afraid to talk on my own telephone? Yesterday I had lunch with a friend of mine whose name you don't need to know. He's in the closet and wants to remain there. Anyway, while we were having lunch I was telling him about this whole mess with Mike's murder, and I happened to mention about his closeted lover being blackmailed. My dear, I thought my friend was going to choke to death! At first, I thought he was Mike's lover, but the truth is worse. My closeted friend has been rather indiscreet. He usually only satisfies his sexual urges when he is outside of New Orleans, but sometimes he calls an escort. He thinks that's safer. Well, he found a young man whom he liked, and called him on several different occasions. He thought the young man knew who he was, but wasn't sure. After his last encounter with the young man, he received a videotape in the mail. It was of the two of them together, and it left no doubt about my friend's particular sexual tastes. The package also contained a request for $50,000 with instructions on where to leave the money. If he didn't pay, everyone that mattered to him would receive a copy of the tape."

"What did he do?"

"He paid, of course." Remy took a deep breath. "When he tried to contact the young man, he'd disappeared. This sounded so like what you told me about Mike's closeted doctor that I thought I should call to let you know. Is this helpful?"

"Very. Thanks, Remy." I hung up the phone. Interesting. There was a blackmail ring in New Orleans targeting closeted wealthy men. But why did they use Mike to black-mail his doctor? Had Mike been in on it and changed his mind later? A hustler. The intruder in my apartment had a list of hustlers' beeper numbers on him.

This was looking less like a hate crime by the minute.

I finished cleaning the apartment. I had time to shower and go by the bank on the way to Paige's. I decided I would pay the hustler for his time. If the paper refused to reim-burse Paige, she wouldn't be out any money for helping me. Besides, if she didn't pay for the hustler, she'd need my permission to run a story on any of this. She wasn't thrilled when I explained it, but she gave in without much of a fight. I think she wasn't sure the paper would pay her back. Even though she's their star reporter, she doesn't earn that much.

The doorbell rang promptly at 2. I answered.

"You're a big one, aren't you?" He was about 5 foot 5. His hair was sandy blond, and he had greenish-blue eyes. His skin was pinkish-brown. The white ribbed tank top and jean shorts he was wearing showed off his nice com-pact body.

"And you are?"

"Trey Lemans is my name, and I'm yours for the next hour." He smiled at me. He couldn't have been 21. He walked in. "Hey, I don't do chicks," he said when he saw Paige. "For no amount of money."

"That's OK, Trey." Paige flashed him a big smile. "I'm not interested."

"I mean, if you want to watch or something, that's cool," he said, pulling off his tank top. His abs were cut perfectly. His entire upper torso was completely hairless. He had a great body, but didn't appeal to me. I don't have anything against shorter guys, but Trey was little more than a kid. His size made him seem even younger.

I shut the front door behind me. "Hate to disappoint you, Trey, but we won't be having sex."

He raised his eyebrows. "You're the one who's missing out, my friend." A worried look came over his face. "Y'all ain't cops?"

Paige patted the sofa next to her invitingly. "No, Trey, we aren't cops. We're just reporters."

"Reporters?"

"I'm doing a story on gay male hustlers." Paige pulled out a tape recorder and switched it on. "We'll pay you your going rate for your time, of course. And we won't use your name in our story if you don't want us to. We'll give you a pseudonym."

"Where's the money?"

I pulled out the wad of bills and handed it to him. He counted it, then put it away. He sat next to Paige. "OK. It's cool, I guess. Ask away."

I sat as well. "How did you become a hustler, Trey?"

He shrugged. "I ran away from home when I was 16. I was born and raised in Placquemines Parish, and that's about all you're going to get out of me about that. My parents were pretty strict. I knew I was gay for as long as I can remember. My mother caught me sucking someone's dick. My father beat me almost to death. I knew I had to get out of there before he killed me. I stole some money from my dad's wallet and I was gone. I came to New Orleans."

"Why New Orleans?" This from Paige.

"Why not New Orleans?" He said. "Everyone knows New Orleans is the place to go if you're gay in Louisiana. It's the only safe place. I knew I could make some money giving blow jobs on the street if I had to."

Oh God, I thought. "And did you?"

"I worked the streets for a couple of years. When I turned 18, I started working at the Pool Cue as a dancer. That helped me get better tricks. That's when I was able to get my first apartment."

Paige's eyes and mine met. The Pool Cue was one of the sleaziest gay bars in New Orleans. The strippers there were rumored to be drug-addicted kids pulled off the streets. "Did you do drugs, Trey?"

"Nah. That's a dead end. But getting that job at the Pool Cue was the best thing that ever happened to me, because if I hadn't been working there, I wouldn't have met Jarrett."

My ears perked up. "Jarrett?"

"Jarrett Phillips. You know, the guy from Gay Rights Now! He was wonderful. He saw me dancing on the bar and asked me if I needed help. I was like, 'Who the fuck is this guy?' But he gave me his business card and told me to call him. I figured he was just some guy who wanted to get in my pants. So I called him, thinking he might be good for a few bucks. The funny thing was, he gave me his card was because he had a group for kids like me. They got me into a nicer apartment, got me into a fitness program, got me eating regularly, and helped me get my GED." He said the last proudly.

"But you're still hustling," Paige said.

Trey shrugged. "It's different. I mean, I could do something else. I'm going to junior college, and then I'm going to UNO. This is the easiest way for me to make money. When Jarrett found out I still wanted to hustle, he introduced me to someone who could help me."

"And who would that be?"

"I'm not going to tell you that." Trey smiled and pulled his tank top back on. "I'm sorry, lady, but I like being a hustler. I know I can't do it forever. That's why I'm going to college. I'm not on drugs, and I've never been arrested — my boss sees to that." He looked at his watch. "And you're out of time. It's been real." And he was out the door.

Paige and I sat in silence for a few moments. "Jarrett Phillips knows someone who runs a male prostitution ring," I said slowly.

"We'll never be able to prove a connection between him and the ring," Paige said, scratching her nose. "I'm sure he's covered those tracks. But he has easy access to prostitutes."

"It's not a long stretch from there to blackmailing some of our city's wealthy and closeted," I replied. "All those anonymous donations — what a neat way to cover up blackmail."

"And maybe murder."

"I think it's time for me to talk to Glen."

CHAPTER TWENTY ONE

I left Paige writing on her computer. I think she was working on Belle. I wasn't sure what to think about anything. I drove on automatic pilot to the Quarter. I had the radio on. It was one of those mindless Top 40 stations where all the music sounds the same. Maybe that's a sign of getting older: The top hits of the week sound exactly the same. This station had two DJs who got high ratings for their stupid banter. It didn't make sense to me. To succeed you appeal to the lowest common denominator.

One of those songs with the nasal-voiced singer whining about something ended. The DJs started their shtick. "Some ruckus in the Quarter last night, huh?"

Number 2 answered, "Well, when you get all those flames together in one spot, you can expect fireworks, I guess."

Number 1 laughed. "Well, according to the news department here at the station, the mayor has called an emergency meeting of the city council and has put a proposition before them about adding gays to the hate-crimes ordinance. What's next, women on their periods?"

I changed to another station. What do two straight assholes know about what it's like to be gay? They didn't have to worry about getting killed because they like women. They don't know what it's like to walk down the street and not be able to hold hands with your date.

I turned onto Magazine. Might as well drive by the house on the way to the Quarter. I wasn't looking forward to meeting with Glen. What was I going to do anyway? Knock on his door and ask him how long he's been a whore?

What right did I have to make judgments on his life?

I liked him.

I was attracted to him.

Hell, I could've just paid him. That would have been that. A business transaction. No emotions. No wondering if he'd want to see me again. All I'd have to do was come up with the cash. Maybe that's the answer to the endless debate about relationships and feelings. When you have the urge, call up an escort. Pay him, enjoy yourself, and send him on his merry way. No unnecessary entanglements. Get your fill and send him home. Was it any different than the way I'd been living until I met Paul? What was the difference? Going to a bar when I was horny, needing to get my rocks off, finding someone hot, making eye contact, starting a conversation, dancing, buying a few drinks, a few furtive kisses on the dance floor, and then back to my place or his for a quick fuck? So no money changed hands in those situations. Maybe that would be better: Sex with a dollar value.

Of course, there's always the "why pay when you can get it for free" argument. *Free. Was it ever free, really?* Free sex meant messing with feelings and emotions.

Feelings and emotions. Was I any different from Glen in all those years since Ryan left me back in college? How many men had I picked up? How many had picked me up? How many of them had I gotten a phone number from and then not called? That was my M.O.—get the sex, get the phone number, move on to the next. Now serving number what? One hundred? Two hundred? Did taking no money make it any better? Was I any less of a whore than Glen?

I stopped in front of my house and got out of the car. I didn't go inside. I sat on the porch to have a smoke. Paul had been leaving messages saying "I love you." I'd been avoiding that entire issue because of the case.

The case. That was a joke. My client was dead. I wasn't getting paid. I was no closer to finding out who the blackmailer was than the day Mike had hired me. Hell, I didn't even know who Mike's lover was! It was all stupid and pointless. I'd been shot at. My apartment had been broken into. Paige had been shot. And for what? All we had were guesses.

Since Ryan had left me, I'd avoided getting involved. I had Paige to hang out with. She was there if I wanted company. It was a 15-minute drive to the Quarter and the bars, if I was horny. You could always get laid in the Quarter. Always. How many men had there been in my bed since Ryan left? Could I even remember them all if I tried? If I wanted to? It was always just sex. Only a few got an encore. I didn't allow it. I never allowed it. That might have gone somewhere.

Hell, I didn't want that many friends. I had Paige. I had Blaine. That was plenty.

Blaine. I sucked in some more smoke and sighed. I'd slept with Blaine more than twice. I'd slept with Blaine quite a few times. Blaine was safe. Blaine wasn't a threat. Blaine had his rich boyfriend whom he wasn't about to leave. It was OK to get naked with him. His boyfriend didn't care. I wasn't a threat to him. So why did I let Paul into my life? Was I able to go that step further? I missed him. I missed him a lot. But why take chances?

A police car parked behind mine. Blaine got out. He looked great, as usual, in his body-hugging uniform. He sat down next to me and rubbed his eyes.

"Were you there last night?" he asked.

"Yeah. Were you?"

He shook his head. "I think you were right to leave the force, Chanse. I think I might have to."

I stared at Blaine in disbelief. Blaine had read me the riot act when I quit. Blaine had always wanted to be a cop. He'd wanted to be a cop when he was a little boy growing up on State Street in the Tujague mansion. His parents had wanted him to be a lawyer or a doctor; he'd wanted to be a cop. He'd studied criminology at Ole Miss, then come back to New Orleans and gone to the police academy. Being a cop was all he'd ever wanted out of life.

He smiled a sad little smile that told me nothing. "They wouldn't let me go down there. They didn't trust me in case of trouble."

"What?"

"Because I'm gay. They didn't trust me to act like a cop if there was trouble." He laughed. "I'm a cop that happens to be gay. I'm not a gay cop. If gays are breaking the law, I'd arrest them like I would anyone else. I was told the other officers going down there for crowd control didn't trust me to back them up."

That must have hurt. "Blaine, I'm sorry."

"You know, you weren't out when you were on the force," he went on. "I mean, if anyone asked you point blank, you'd tell them, but most guys didn't believe it. I mean, you were the football player from LSU—how could you be a faggot? Me, though, I'm from Uptown. Uptown boys don't become cops. And I've always been out. I put up with a lot of shit proving myself to the force. See how much trust I've earned. Wow." A tear rolled out of his left eye.

"What'll you do if you quit?"

He shrugged. "Who knows? I don't have to work. Todd points that out every time I turn around. He's got money and I've never touched my trust fund. I guess I could go back to school, get a master's or something." He wiped the tear off his cheek. "All I've ever wanted was to be a cop."

"Well, this is no reason to give up." I thought about putting my arm around him. Not a good idea. No telling who might be driving by. Camp Street is always pretty busy. "You're just hurt. This whole thing's got everyone acting weird."

"Yeah. Whatever. Maybe I'll just take some time off." He leaned back against one of the posts. "Paige doing OK?"

"Yeah, she's fine." I looked at him. "Let me ask you something. Have you ever been with an escort?"

"I don't pay for sex."

"That's not an answer."

Blaine stared at me. "No, I haven't. Escorts are for guys that can't get laid. Why?"

"No reason."

He grinned. "You found out about Glen Chandler, didn't you?"

It was my turn to stare at him. "How did you know?"

"Not how you think." He laughed. "Glen tried to recruit me one night at the Pub when Todd was out of town. Glen's a hot little number, and he looked like fun. You should've seen the look on his face when I told him I was a cop!"

"He tried to recruit you?"

Blaine was grinning from ear to ear. "Yeah. He said he knew a way for a guy as hot as me to make a lot of money. I asked how, and he told me. That's when I told him I was a cop. I thought he was going to wet himself."

"Why didn't you tell me he was an escort?"

"I didn't think you were going to fuck him." He looked at me closely. "I mean, I figured you and Paul had a good thing going, and you wouldn't mess that up, right?"

"I didn't sleep with him, no." *But you wanted to,* I told myself. *Isn't that what matters?*

"I bet he's good. Have you ever seen him dance?" Blaine winked at me. "He can move that body on the dance floor. If he can fuck the way he dances, he's be worth every penny he charges." He stood. "Well, I need to get back to the station. Call you later, OK?"

"Yeah." I watched him drive off down Camp Street. How many people in New Orleans knew Glen was out for hire?

I drove to the Quarter. Tourists were clogging the streets. I parked on Burgundy and walked over to Glen's. I rang the bell. Before long, I heard footsteps. "Who is it?" Glen asked in a low voice.

"It's me, Chanse."

He unlatched the gate and opened it. His face was a mess. The entire left side of his face looked as though he had been playing chicken with an 18-wheeler and lost. It was various shades of green, blue, and purple. His left eye was swollen and bloodshot. His upper lip was swollen. He smiled weakly. "Not pretty, huh?"

I resisted the urge to take him in my arms and hold him. "You OK?"

"Surviving," he said. "Come in."

I followed him down that narrow passage to the court-yard and up the stairs. "Something to drink?" he asked as I sat on the couch.

"No thanks."

He sat beside me and put his hand on my leg. "I'm glad you're here."

No sense in beating around the bush. "So how long have you been an escort?"

He flinched. "You found out."

"Well?"

"It's none of your business." He turned away from me. "You can leave if you want to."

"I want to know why."

He looked at me again, eyes flashing. "Why? So you can judge me? So you can think I'm a whore?"

"So I can understand." I knew it was true when I said it. I wanted to know why an attractive, intelligent guy like Glen would sell his body.

"It was flattering to be asked," he said. "Don't make that face at me! You don't understand what my life was like, do you? Of course you wouldn't. You've always been a jock, a great big good-looking guy with muscles that everyone wants to have. Have you ever thought about what it's like to be fat? To go into a bar and be laughed at? To hear some bitchy queen with the IQ of a doorknob but the body of a god say, 'Look at that troll!' and know they're talking about you? Do you know what it's like to have some great-looking guy start talking to you only to find out that he's an escort and you look desperate enough to pay for sex? Do you have any idea what it's like to be a good person—a nice guy—

and get treated like a leper because you're overweight? No, I don't think you do."

"What does that have to do with it?"

"People pay me for sex," Glen said. "A year ago, nobody would give me the time of day, let alone a second glance. Now I can walk into a bar and have my choice of men. Men pay me for sex."

"Did Mike know?"

"What does Mike have to do with this?" Glen lit a cigarette and blew smoke at me.

I shrugged. "Just curious."

"You want to know if I ever rubbed his face in it?" Glen said. "Mike introduced me to the man who got me started, if you must know."

"And who was that?"

"Answer a question for me." Glen crossed his legs. "How did you find out?"

"I called a beeper number for an escort, and you called back. Who got you started?"

"How did you get my beeper number?"

"That doesn't matter."

He threw up his arms in the air. "Abel Fontenot. He approached me one night at the Parade and asked if I was interested in making extra money. I needed a computer, and my Transco salary wasn't going pay for one anytime soon. So I said sure, as long as it didn't involve selling drugs or anything."

Nice to know he drew the line somewhere. "And you don't mind being a whore?"

His eyes narrowed. "Go to hell, Chanse. Just go to hell. I don't need you to judge me, OK? I don't see how we're that different. You're a whore too, only I'm honest enough to take money for it."

"I sleep with people I like—not whoever has the cash." I walked to the door.

"Why are you so judgmental?" He followed me to the door. "I mean, I thought you were different. I liked you, Chanse."

"I'm sorry, Glen. I just don't think I can afford you." I walked outside.

The door slammed behind me.

CHAPTER TWENTY-TWO

Who was I to judge Glen? I tried to imagine what it would be like to walk into Oz 30 pounds overweight. Yeah, they would laugh. The pretty boys with the big muscles would avoid eye contact. They'd move away from you. No one would talk to you. It would be rough. It would hurt. Maybe it did make a warped kind of sense for Glen to become a whore.

It was just something I knew I couldn't do.

Besides, was it different from Justin's arrangement with Remy? Mike's with his closet case?

There were no messages when I got home. *OK, fine.* I got a Dr. Pepper. I'd just sat on the couch when I heard the squeak of the front gate opening. Probably just the mailman. My doorbell rang.

I looked through the blinds. It was Yvonne from GRN.

I opened the door. "Hey, Yvonne."

She seemed agitated. She kept looking back at the street. "Can I please come in?"

I stood aside to let her in. "What's up?"

She sat on the couch. She pulled out a cigarette and lit it. Her hands were shaking. "I'm scared."

Oh, Lord. "Of what?"

She took a deep breath. "Something's going on at GRN. Something wrong." She reached into her purse and pulled out a videocassette. "I found this in Jarrett's office before I left last night. I went home and watched it."

Yvonne turned the tape over so that the label showed: *Gold Mine.* She handed the tape to me. "What is it?" I asked.

"You'll have to watch it to believe it."

I turned on the television and popped the tape into my VCR. I hit play. Blue screen giving way to fuzz. *OK, what was this?* A picture came into focus. I realized I was look-ing through Mike's living room window. There was a man standing with his back to the camera. Mike's sofa had been folded out into a bed. I could see a muscular leg hanging off one side. It looked like Mike's. I leaned forward. The man with his back to the camera started removing his shirt. His back was tanned and muscled. His salt-and-pepper hair was cut short. He undid his pants and stepped out of them. Underneath, all he had on was a pair of white jockeys. I was impressed by how he looked in them. Nice strong legs led up to a nice round ass. Two hands came from around the front of him and slid the jockeys down. He moved to the side of the bed. Mike was lying on the bed completely naked. I whistled. No wonder Ronnie Bishop wasn't ready to let go of him. Mike could have been a major porn star. I still couldn't see the face of the man with him. Mike stood. The man bent down, and they kissed. The guy was at least six inches taller than Mike. Mike turned his back to the camera and knelt in front of him. The man's face moved into camera range.

My eyes about fell out of my head.

I hit the freeze button on my VCR remote and stared at the television screen. There was no doubt about it.

I stopped the tape and hit rewind. There it was. Proof

positive that Bryce was Mike's closeted lover.

"My God." I looked at Yvonne. She was on her third cigarette.

"Chanse, I'm scared. I didn't know what to do with that tape. I thought about going to the police, but…" Her voice trailed off.

"Jarrett could just deny that he'd ever seen it. It would be your word against his." I scratched my head.

"If he knew I had that tape…oh, God." She buried her face in her hands.

"Why did you take it?"

"Like I said, there's something weird going on. I mean, ever since Mike was killed, Jarrett's been having all of these private hush-hush meetings with Abel Fontenot. Usually, he records all of his meetings and has me type them up. But he hasn't been taping his meetings with Abel lately. And he's been getting weird phone calls."

"From who?"

She held up her hands. "I don't know. Usually, Jarrett won't take a call unless I find out who it is first. He's been taking these."

"How long has this been going on?"

"The first one was on the day Mike was killed. I'd just gotten back from lunch. It was a man. He was terribly upset. He wanted to talk to Jarrett but wouldn't give me his name. When I told him that I had to have a name, he just said, 'Tell him it's *Gold Mine.*' Jarrett took the call. So when I saw this tape lying on Jarrett's desk marked *Gold Mine,* I took it."

"Abel Fontenot is GRN's development director, isn't he?"

"Yes. He's in charge of fund-raising."

Fund-raising.

Male escorts.

Blackmail.

I closed my eyes. They hire male escorts and put them to work. The escorts report back on who their clients are. Once in a while they land one who's rich and closeted. Abel and Jarrett make a tape of the next session. Presto— a failing nonprofit is flourishing.

"Abel scares me," Yvonne said, her voice shaking. "I think he likes to hurt people."

"Why do you say that?"

"Just the way he looks at me sometime, like he's imagining how much pain I can handle, or something. I've heard stories about him at the bar...." She stopped and hugged herself.

"Yvonne, are you aware that Abel runs a ring of male escorts?"

She shook her head. "No." She looked at her watch. "I've got to run, Chanse. Please don't tell anyone where you got that tape, OK?"

After she'd gone, I got out the yellow pages and looked up Bryce Dubuisson's office number. I dialed it. "Dr. Dubuisson, please." I said when someone answered.

"May I ask who's calling?" the voice replied.

"Chanse MacLeod. Tell him it's about Mike." I was put on hold, listening to an old Air Supply song about getting lost in love. Sentimental crap. Lost in love. Please.

"Dr. Dubuisson."

"Good afternoon, Doctor, I'm sorry to disturb you, but—"

"Why are you harassing me? I already told you that I didn't know Mike Hansen."

"Yes, yes, that's right. Anyway, I have something here that you might want to see."

"I doubt that very seriously."

"Right now, I'm watching you and Mike. On videotape. Do you know what I mean?"

There was silence. "What do you want? Money?"

"I just want to talk to you. When is your last patient?"

"I just finished with her."

"Come over to my apartment. We need to talk." I gave him directions and hung up.

I called Paige, but all I got was her voice mail. I left her a quick message.

A few minutes later my doorbell rang. I checked through the blinds. A silver Lexus was parked at the curb. It was Bryce, all right. I opened the door.

"Is my car safe here?" He asked nervously.

I shrugged. "I guess."

"Look, I'm not paying any more money to anyone." He folded his arms. "I've already paid twice, OK? I'm not paying again."

"Slow down, Bryce." I gestured for him to sit. "I don't want money from you. As far as I'm concerned, if you want to stay in the closet, you can. Not my business. I'm trying to find out who killed Mike."

Bryce sighed. His eyes were wet. "Oh, God."

"Bryce, what the hell was going on with you and Mike?"

"We were in love." He laughed, shaking his head. "Sounds crazy, doesn't it? It's a long story."

"I've got lots of time."

"For someone like you, it's hard to understand the choices that I've made in my life." He rubbed his eyes. "I always knew, from when I was a little boy, that I liked boys better than girls. But I was a Dubuisson. The only son. I had to carry on the family name. My father is a homophobe, Chanse. When I was 17, he caught me with one of the gardeners. It was one of the most horrible moments of my life. The gardener, of course, was fired on the spot."

"And?"

"I was called into my father's study. I was told that such behavior for a Dubuisson was completely unacceptable. That if I wanted to continue with such perverted behavior, he would write me a check for $10,000, and I could pack up my things and get out of his house and never return. There would be no medical school. My trust fund would be closed. As far as he was concerned, I would cease to exist. I would have to change my name, because he would not allow me to live as a pervert with the Dubuisson name."

"Sounds pretty awful."

"What was I supposed to do? I suppose I could have called his bluff, but I was only 17. I couldn't imagine giving up the house, the krewes, the money, for what? To have sex with men? No, I think I made the right decision. I agreed to my father's conditions. The subject was closed."

"But you kept sleeping with men, didn't you?"

He nodded. "I couldn't help myself. It was always out of town. I couldn't take the chance someone might find out. You know how this town thrives on gossip." He laughed bitterly. "I met Mike at a gay bar in Pensacola. I was there for a medical conference. I decided to go out and have some fun. He was there, with no shirt on and shorts that might have been illegal. His body should've been against the law. I bought him a drink, one thing led to another, and he went back to my hotel with me. Mike was an incredible lover. Mind if I smoke?" I'm always amazed by how many doctors smoke. "Imagine my shock a few months later when I ran into him in the French Quarter."

"And?"

"Things are different now." He took a deep breath. "I've never lied to my wife, Chanse. She's always known that I'm gay. She doesn't care. We have an agreement. Once my father is dead, we are getting divorced. I'm going to be able to live the life that I want. She'll live in the mansion. My father has maybe a few months to live, tops. I decided to take a chance on this guy. I started seeing him. Mike knew I was married and that we had to keep it a secret. I started falling in love with him."

Interesting. Was this the person who'd say something nice about Mike? "You loved him?"

He laughed. "A lot of people hated him. He knew it. He told me about how he treated people. He was honest with me. I knew all about Remy Deveraux and his lover."

"You didn't care that he slept with other people?"

"As long as he was safe." Bryce looked at me. "I couldn't offer him anything except money or love until my father died. I couldn't ask him for anything."

"Did he ask for money?"

"No. He didn't want our relationship to be based on financial need."

"How could you trust him, Dr. Dubuisson? Knowing what he was doing to people like Remy and Justin? Weren't you afraid that he might be yanking your chain?"

"I'm telling you intimate details of my private life. The least you can do is call me Bryce," he said. "People treated

Mike like a piece of meat. Ronnie Bishop certainly did. Mike showed me some letters Ronnie wrote him after they broke up—all this talk about Mike's body and what a fantastic lover he was. He was just a fuck to Ronnie Bishop. That's how most people treated him. I didn't. I treated him like a person. I wanted to know what he wanted to do with his life—what his dreams were. No one else asked him things like that. Yeah, Mike treated people badly, but he was treated badly himself. How would you feel if people only wanted to be friends with you to get you into bed?"

"That would be shitty." It was the opposite end of the coin from Glen. Glen felt like a nonentity because he'd been fat; Mike felt like a nonentity because he was beautiful. Weird.

"So he felt free to treat people badly when they acted like he was just a sex object. I'm not saying it was right, but I couldn't blame him. These people gave him the power to treat them that way. He hoped they'd learn a lesson from it. He told me once they probably just called him a bitch and went along on their merry little way."

"He was right about that at least," I replied. The ones I'd talked to felt that way.

"I knew Mike wasn't behind the tape when it came in the mail. He worried because they wanted money. Fifty thousand dollars, or they were going to send it to my father." He sighed. "I got the money in cash and followed their instructions."

"Which were?"

"I was supposed to put the money in a briefcase and the briefcase in a locker at the airport. The blackmailer had sent me a key to use. I put the key in an envelope and left it at the airport lost and found."

"What guarantee did you have they wouldn't ask for more?"

"None," he said bitterly. "I figured I was going to have to keep paying until my father died, at which point it would be over."

"What did Mike think about this?"

"Mike was angry. He told me he was going to hire a private detective and get to the bottom of it. Then he was killed."

I didn't ask him why he didn't go to the police. He couldn't, not without revealing his connection with Mike. "Well, he did hire a detective. He hired me."

He looked at me in surprise. "Why didn't he tell me?"

"He hired me the day he was murdered. I found his body when I went to keep an appointment with him. He was going to show me the tape. But when the police searched the apartment, they didn't find it."

"So that's why he came and got the tape from me," he said. "I wondered about that. When he was killed I was terrified the police would find it. And then I got another demand in the mail the day he died. With another tape. This time I had to put $50,000 in a briefcase and leave it at the lost-and-found at Jax Brewery."

"Mike's death wasn't a hate crime, Bryce. He was killed because of that tape." I looked at him. "You do realize that you're a suspect?"

He shook his head. "I was seeing patients when Mike was killed. I didn't even take a lunch break. I have dozens of people who can verify that."

I nodded. I hadn't taken him seriously as a suspect. I doubted that Venus would either.

"Chanse, if you put a stop to this once and for all for me, I'll pay you the $50,000."

That gave me pause. $50,000? I wouldn't have to work for a year. I smiled. "You've got a deal, Bryce."

CHAPTER TWENTY-THREE

Finally, a paying client.

It might not have been completely ethical to accept Bryce's offer. After all, I'd already been investigating the entire thing, and I was almost positive I knew who the blackmailers were. But my time is valuable. It wasn't like Bryce couldn't afford it. Fifty thousand dollars was a lot more than my going rate. A lot more. But hey, I'd been shot at, my apartment had broken into, and my best friend had been shot. I felt entitled. Besides, it was his idea. He wrote me a retainer check for $5,000 and went home. Once he left, I called Yvonne.

I wasn't really sure what my game plan was going to be. I was pretty certain that Mike's death was related to Jarrett's blackmail ring but had no proof. No way to connect it to Jarrett. I doubted he'd confess. Yvonne's word that she found the tape in his office would mean nothing in New Orleans's racist, corrupt justice system. I needed something concrete. Like a murder weapon. There had to be something in Jarrett's office. If I could find something to connect him to the blackmail ring, he might break on the murder. Abel Fontenot was probably the shooter, but the orders had to have come from Jarrett.

I met Yvonne at Kaldi's as night was falling. She was nervous. "I don't know about this, Chanse."

"Yvonne, you know as well as I do that that tape links Jarrett and Abel to Mike's murder."

"What if you get caught?"

"You said yourself that Abel and Jarrett were meeting with the city council tonight." I smiled at her. I needed a cigarette.

"OK." She slipped a key off her ring. She wrote a number down on the back of a business card. "That's the alarm code. The alarm setting is on the wall right inside the front door." She stood. "I'll need the key back tonight."

"I'll be back by midnight." A thought occurred to me. "If you haven't heard from me by then, call my friend Paige. She'll know what to do." I wrote the number down.

"I hope you don't find anything." She walked out.

I waited another half-hour before walking down toward the Marigny. It was dark. Decatur Street was alive with people. I crossed over into the Marigny. I walked up French-men Street. Washington Square was deserted. I waited for a few cars to go by. I unlocked the door to Gay Rights Now! and shut off the alarm. I pulled out my pocket flashlight. I entered Jarrett's office.

I started with his desk. Sure enough, in the top drawer were the keys to the file cabinet. Right where Yvonne had said they would be. I walked over to the first one and unlocked it. I started going through the files.

It took about an hour before I found anything.

In the bottom drawer of an unmarked cabinet, I found a treasure trove of tapes. I picked one up and shined the flashlight at it. I recognized the name on the label. A former King of Rex. A well-respected lawyer and family man. I shined the light on some of the others. The ones that I recognized were all married, wealthy men. I let out a low whistle. "Well, well, well." Now all I had to do was find something to connect Jarrett and Abel to Mike.

My stomach flipped when the light turned on.

"What are you doing in here?"

I turned around. It was Abel Fontenot. He looked the same as he had at Brian's gallery, with one difference. In his right hand he held a gun. "Hey, Abel."

"Put your hands up." I complied. My pulse was racing. This was not good. He walked toward me carefully and looked into the drawer. "Shit."

"Does Jarrett know you keep your porn collection in his office?"

"Shut the fuck up!" He punched me in the stomach. Hard. I didn't see it coming. I doubled over. I tried to catch my breath. He'd pay for that one. "Sit over there!" He gestured to a chair. I walked over to it and sat down. He went over to a closet and got out some rope. I didn't want to know why Jarrett kept rope in his closet. He bound my hands to the chair. Tight. It hurt. He then tied my ankles together. Tighter. If I got out of this, I was going to kick his ass. He gagged me as well. He was good with knots.

He left the room and turned the light off.

I've never been fond of the dark.

I pulled against the ropes. They were tight. There was no leeway at all. The chair was on rollers. I tried to roll it, but my feet were tied too tight. I couldn't move the chair. Abel was good at tying people up.

This was not good.

They were going to kill me.

No reason to let me live. If they killed Mike, they'd kill me for sure.

The door opened. The light came on. "Son of a bitch!" I recognized Jarrett's voice.

"I told you. What, you thought I was lying?" Abel said.

Jarrett came around to the front of me. "You're sure he saw the tapes?"

"The drawer's still open."

Jarrett sighed. "Well, you know what to do."

Everything went dark.

I came to hearing the chugging sound of an engine. I opened my eyes. I was gagged, my mouth was dry, my head hurt. I was staring up at the sky. It was dark. The stars were out. I tried to sit up. My hands were tied behind my back. My ankles were tied together. I pushed myself up into a sitting position. I was in the back of a boat. I could make out the shapes of two men in the cabin. I strained my neck to try to see over the side. Was this the river, the lake, or the swamp? I couldn't see shore or trees in either direction. Just wide expanses of still water. The lake.

They were going to dump me into the lake, tied up.

I can't swim.

My mind flashed back to my childhood. My parents had taken my sister and me to the river one summer to teach us how to swim. They had sat there, getting drunk on Pearl beer, while the two of splashed in the dirty water. After a few hours, when our skin was turning red from the sun, my father had staggered down, picked us up in the crook of his arms, and carried us out to where the water was deeper. He pitched us out. "Swim!" he shouted. My sister and I had both been terrified. The current was much faster out in the deep. I tried to keep my head above water. My sister kept screaming. I refused to scream, to give my father that satisfaction.

Several times as I sank beneath the surface, I thought that maybe it would be better not to try to go back to the surface. Just stay down there and keep swallowing water. Anything was better than going back. My lungs began to ache as I sank deeper in the dirty river. I began to feel light-headed. I began to black out as hands grabbed me and pushed toward to the surface. It was my father. He pulled me into the shallow water and started beating me. "Useless little pansy!" he screamed, the sour smell of beer almost making me gag. "Even a fucking dog can swim!" he screamed, beating me as I choked and gagged on regurgitated water.

"Even a fucking dog can swim."

Not with its paws tied together.

It was getting darker as the boat continued to chug its way out farther from shore. I was going to die, no doubt about it. Would they just let me drown, or would they shoot me and weight the body? A plane had crashed into Lake Pontchartrain once, an Eastern jet with a full load of passengers. It had never been recovered, not a piece of it, not a single body. Lake Pontchartrain is cold and deep and rarely gives up its secrets. It's pretty easy to dispose of bodies in New Orleans. There's the lake. There's the river with its strong current carrying bodies right out to the gulf. I guess I should have been grateful that they had chosen the lake over the swamp. The lake was too polluted for alligators.

I pulled at the ropes on my wrists. There were too tight. I wondered idly if Abel was into bondage.

How long would it be before I was missed? A couple of days? Paige would be pissed that I wasn't returning her calls. Paul wasn't due back for a couple of days. That's probably what it would take: Paul coming back into town and not being met at the airport. He would take a cab to my apartment, let himself in with the key, and notice the answering machine with about 20 messages from Paige. He would call Paige, and then the worry would begin. Or maybe Yvonne would call Paige and tell her what was up when I didn't return her key at midnight.

Either way, my body would never be found, unless by some fluke, and by that time the fish would have been at me. I would be a John Doe. Jarrett and Abel would get away with this. Mike's murder would go unsolved because I had stupidly never given Venus the tip about the escorts. Bryce Dubuisson wouldn't come forward, not as long as his father was alive, unless they tried to blackmail him again. Then again, they could always just kill Bryce too.

I closed my eyes. This truly sucked.

I'd never thought much about death, except to know that I didn't want to die. I don't believe in God and the afterlife. Growing up with my parents convinced me that hell is actually a place on earth. My mind couldn't comprehend the possibility that there was something worse after death. Besides, I was gay, and every Christian that I knew thought that because of that I was destined for their hell. Of course, to me the thought of hell was spending eternity being preached at by Christians, so I would probably end up in their heaven as my hell. Terrific.

The boat stopped moving, the engine stilled. *Well, this is it,* I thought, and sent a mental apology to Paul. *Sorry to die on you this way, Paul.*

Abel and Jarrett came back to where I was propped up. Abel pulled the gag down. I croaked, "So, what's the plan, boys?" through dry lips with a bravado I didn't feel. I'd be damned if I would beg the bastards for my life.

"Dump him overboard, Abel," Jarrett said. He knelt by me. "I'm really sorry about this, Chanse. I didn't want anyone to be hurt. But I can't let you put an end to all the good work GRN has done. I just can't."

"Why did you kill Mike?"

He shook his head. "I didn't kill Mike."

"Why did you have him killed then?"

He laughed, a bit sadly. "I had nothing to do with Mike's death, Chanse. I know you find that hard to believe, especially since I'm about to kill you, but I didn't. I wanted Mike to be one of our escorts. I admit that, but I didn't kill him, nor did I want him dead." He stood. "Over the side with him."

Abel picked me up like I was a sack of garbage. I weigh 220, so that was no small feat. He carried me to the side of the boat, and then I went over.

The lake was cold. I took a deep breath as I hit the water and held it as I sank. I opened my eyes and could barely make out the hull of the boat. I could see the motor blades. I tried kicking with my legs, but with the ankles tied, I made little progress. I kept moving up, my lungs ready to burst, swearing at myself for not giving up cigarettes, for smoking pot every day. My head broke the surface, and I desperately gulped for air before I sank beneath the surface again. Without being able to use my arms, I couldn't stay up. My legs were getting tired as I sank beneath the surface again. I stopped moving them to let them rest, and I started sinking again.

"Can't you even float?" I heard my father screaming at me.

Float.

I kicked upward, breaking the surface. I gasped air in, and then arched my back. My chest and stomach rose to the top of the water. I bobbed there, water covering my face and then clearing. I could hear the engine of the boat chugging away in the distance. They hadn't shot me. They hadn't shot at me.

I could survive this.

The water was cold. My arms, floating limply underneath me, were going numb. I let my pelvis drop a bit and then straightened out again, kicking downward with my legs. I managed to move a few feet through the water. Cool. I carefully turned my head from side to side. There was no sign of shore in either direction. There was no way of telling what direction I was moving either. But as long as I could keep moving, I knew I was still alive. I tried again, and moved again. Cool. As long as my muscles held out, I would keep moving. I just hoped I wasn't going sideways down the length of the lake. Of course, the lake is about 30 miles wide as well, but I pushed that thought down in my head. I was going to make it. I kept moving.

My mind wandered as I moved. More stars came out. My arms were tingling. The water was damned cold, but as long as I moved, I was fine. I could almost feel the blood circulating. Fortunately, there was no wind. Waves would have been the death of me. I started thinking about things, anything to keep my mind alive and alert. I remembered the day Mike approached me at the gym. I remembered going by his apartment, finding the body. Jarrett was so insistent that he hadn't killed Mike or been responsible for his death. Well, who was then? I mean, why would Jarrett lie to me? I was as good as dead, anyway. Would it have hurt him to confess? He'd confessed to the blackmail readily enough.

He was about to leave me for dead in the middle of Lake Pontchartrain. So it stood to reason that he hadn't killed Mike. Great. Something he was innocent of.

OK, think.

How had they gotten the tape of Mike and Bryce? Jarrett had said that Mike wasn't one of their escorts. Glen had said the same thing. So how had the tape been made? It wasn't made with Mike's knowledge, or he wouldn't have hired me. Bryce had been willing to pay the money. Mike had insisted on hiring me. Mike had been a mercenary son of a bitch, but he hadn't been willing to share Bryce's money with anyone.

So how had they gotten the tape?

Something was nagging at me. There was something there. The tape was the key.

My legs were getting tired. I took a deep breath and just stayed there, floating. I couldn't fall asleep. That would be death for sure. I was exhausted. I rested for a while, then started moving again. My legs ached. My arms were dead. My breath was coming in ragged little gasps, but somehow I kept going.

I started to hallucinate.

I saw my father.

I could smell him.

"Even a fucking dog can swim!"

Paul's voice: *"I love you."*

Paige: *"Come on, Chanse."*

Mike's voice: *"You were a football player."*

I rammed into something, and pain shot through my shoulder. I sank beneath the surface again. Exhausted, tired, I summoned the energy to kick back up to the top.

An oil rig.

I had run into one of the lake wells.

I propelled myself over to it again. I allowed my legs to drop down, trying to find a foothold. It took my three tries, but finally got my feet onto one of the crossbeams. I leaned into it, breathing hard. It was a working well. I could feel the vibrations of the pump at the lake bottom. How often did they come out to check the wells? Did they ever? I started shivering, and rested. My legs felt like they were going to fall right out of the hip joint. My arms had ceased to feel a long time before. How long had I been out there? There was no way of telling. My watch was on my wrist, but my wrists were behind my back. I stood there until my breathing became more even, until my lungs stopped hurting.

I lost my balance and slid into one of the uprights. Feeling in my right arm came back in a rush of pain. It was sharp. I could feel blood trickling down my arm.

Hope came back to me in a rush of energy. The upright was sharp! I positioned myself so it was between my arms, balanced on one foot. I started moving my arms up and down. I could feel the tension on the ropes. I kept sawing, trying to keep my balance. The sky was starting to lighten when the rope finally cut in half. I was so startled that I lost my balance and fell headfirst into the lake. As I sank, I struggled with the ropes on my wrists. They finally fell away. I used my arms to propel me back up. I grabbed onto the rig with both hands and pulled myself up. Now to free my legs.

The ropes were wet. My hands and fingers numb. I was sitting on a crossbar when I heard, "What the fuck?" I still thought I was hallucinating, so I ignored it.

"What the fuck are you doing?"

I looked down and saw a small fishing boat with two men in it.

"You wouldn't believe me if I told you," I said weakly.

And fell back into the water.

CHAPTER TWENTY-FOUR

Luck has a lot to do with whether you're successful in my line of work. I've always been pretty lucky. I was alive only because two guys decided to call in sick for work and go fishing. What they were expecting to catch that would be edible, I don't know. I don't ask questions when I get that lucky.

I wasn't lucky enough to avoid the hospital. Shots. Tests. Overnight observation. Whatever. It was going to cost me a pretty penny once the bill came. I didn't want to stay overnight, but Paige and Venus overruled me. I'd sworn out a statement for Venus in my hospital room between tests. She was more than happy to run a warrant for the arrest of Jarrett Phillips and Abel Fontenot on charges of attempted murder. Venus was also sure that one or both of them had killed Mike. She didn't listen to my theories. Once she was gone, Paige looked at me thoughtfully. "Why do you think Jarrett didn't kill Mike?"

"It just seems to me that at that point he would have nothing to lose by admitting it," I said. "He was about to feed me to the fishes. Why not admit it?"

"That's not evidence."

"I know." I yawned. They had given me sedatives. Every muscle in my body was aching. My ass was sore from shots.

"Get some sleep," she said.

I did. I slept the rest of that day and night. They released me the next morning. Paige dropped me off at my apartment. The apartment seemed surreal. I'd thought I'd never see it again. There were no messages on the machine. I sat for a while. My couch felt good. I closed my eyes. Then it came to me.

I drove to the Quarter. The answer had been staring me in the face. I parked on Ursulines and walked up Dauphine to Mike's apartment building. I rang Glen's buzzer. I heard him coming down the narrow passage. The gate opened.

He frowned. "Did you come to preach at me some more?"

"No, I just need to check something out with Mike's apartment."

He let me pass. I walked back into the courtyard. The yellow crime-scene tape was still around the door to Mike's apartment. I walked over to the living room window, and I looked in. Yes, this was the right angle for the tape. I turned and looked at the brick fence. There was about three feet between the window and the fence. The fence was higher than my head. Broken glass was imbedded in the cement at the top. It could not have been shot from anywhere else.

Glen had gone back up to his apartment. I climbed the steps and knocked on his door. He opened it. "What?"

"I need to talk to you." I pushed past him into the apartment. I looked around in the living room. New stereo. New computer. All the electronic equipment in his apartment was new.

"I have to go to work in a hour."

"This won't take long." I faced him in the middle of the room. "Was it your idea or Jarrett's to videotape Mike and Bryce?"

"What?" His face drained of color. "That's insane!"

"Is it?" I folded my arms. "The video was shot through Mike's living room window. The fence is too high for it to have been shot from anywhere else. The only people with access to the courtyard were you, Mike, and your landlord. Your landlord has been in France for three months. Mike didn't shoot the tape. That leaves you."

"I don't have to listen to this bullshit." He pointed at the door. "Get out!"

"There were two different attempts to blackmail Bryce," I said. "The first was undoubtedly Jarrett. But the second attempt was completely different from the first. Like there were two different people blackmailing Bryce." I walked over to the entertainment center. "New stereo. New VCR. New television."

"I make a lot of money escorting."

I walked over to the desk. "New computer too. Escorting certainly pays well."

"Get out!"

"You know, the police are looking for Jarrett and Abel," I went on. "Once they're caught, they're not going to cover for you. How did they find out that you'd blackmailed Bryce on your own? That's who beat you up, isn't it? Abel Fontenot? Not some gay bashers running around?"

He took a deep breath and sat on the couch. "It was Abel. He called Bryce to see about getting more money out of him, and that's when he found out that Bryce had already paid twice. I didn't think they'd call him again. I mean, why not? I kept a copy of the tape."

"Did you beat off watching Mike and Bryce getting it on? Is that why you kept a copy?"

He buried his face in his hands. "Oh, God."

"Why did you kill him?"

He looked up. "I didn't kill Mike."

"Yes, Glen, you did." I knelt in front of him. "Why?"

He looked up at me. He was crying. "He figured it out. He knew who shot the tape. Before he came home that day, he'd gotten the tape from Bryce. He watched it. Then he called me to come down. I had no idea. When I got down there, he turned the tape on and asked me why I'd done it. I denied it. He said that I was the only one who could have made the tape, or I knew who had. He pulled a gun out. He was going to call the police. We fought over the gun. It went off. He died. I didn't know what to do. I called Jarrett, told him everything. He told me what to do, about writing on the wall and everything. He was going to come by on the pretext of finding the body. That's why the gate was open. I'd left it open for him. Oh, God."

"The night we were shot at?"

"I called Abel from the coffee shop. He just cruised around waiting for us. It was supposed to be a warning to you. They promised they wouldn't hurt you."

I wanted to punch him. *"They promised." My ass.* They had broken into my apartment and shot Paige. I walked over to the telephone.

"What are you doing?"

"I'm calling the police."

"You can't!" He got up and walked toward me. "Please, Chanse, I can't go to jail. I just can't."

"I'm sorry, Glen." I started dialing. "I'm calling the police." I heard Venus answer. Before I could say anything, he was on me. The phone clattered out of my hand onto the floor.

He knocked me back into the wall. I shouted Venus's name, and then his hands were on my neck, choking. He was very strong. I managed to get my arms up and knock him back. I reached for the phone, and he kicked me in the side of the head. I saw stars, heard bells, and staggered back into the foyer. I looked up in time to see him grab a wicked-looking knife out of the knife rack. I stepped backwards. He swung the knife at me. I dodged, my head still buzzing. He lunged again, and I grabbed for the arm holding the knife. I got a hold of him, and he struggled back, trying to shove the knife into my chest. With his free hand he tried to claw at my eyes. We backed up against the wall. He pulled free of my hands and swung the knife back. I looked into his eyes. They were crazed. He swung the knife back at me. I stepped aside and grabbed the arm and used his momentum to swing him around, but he slipped out of my grasp and crashed through the glass door. His momentum carried him backward across the porch and into the railing, which gave way behind his weight.

There was a thud as he hit the pavement of the courtyard.

Gasping for breath, I stepped through the shattered glass door and looked down at him. Blood was spreading underneath his head.

I sank down on the porch, trying to catch my breath.

In the distance, I heard the wail of sirens.

I pulled my pocket tape recorder out of my pants pocket and switched it off.

The police haven't caught Abel or Jarrett. The morning after they dumped me in the lake, they emptied GRN's accounts and vanished. Jarrett is not a stupid man. I'm sure he's probably sitting on an island somewhere in the Caribbean, having a drink and seducing young island boys.

The police and the district attorney's office chose not to make public the whole truth about what had been going on at GRN. Instead, the scandal broke as simple embezzlement. The story that was released was that Glen had killed Mike in a lover's quarrel. Bryce was quite relieved. He paid me the $50,000 he'd promised. It's sitting at the Whitney Bank in a CD that rolls over weekly.

Paige chose to stick with the story the police offered, even though she didn't believe it for a minute. When she got the real story out of me (aided by some pot and wine), she didn't push it. Her arm is healing nicely, although there'll be a scar.

Blaine decided to stay with the police force. If anyone was born to serve and protect, it was Blaine. Being a cop is all he ever wanted, and he'd be lost without that. Even though Todd hates for him to be a cop, he was the one who talked him into staying on the force.

The ordinance in front of the city council that Jarrett worked so hard for—including gays and lesbians in the city's hate-crimes law—passed by a very close vote. Within days, the conservatives had rallied enough support to put it to a vote by the citizens of the city. I would like to say the city voted to keep it on the books, but it was defeated 63% to 37%. But that's progress of a sort. Paige pointed out that in a citywide poll taken in New Orleans several years ago, 74% had been in favor of upholding Louisiana's sodomy law.

I don't feel quite as unsafe walking the streets anymore. I'll never feel as completely safe as I did before Mike Hansen hired me, but I'm getting better.

Paul and I are going a little slow. I care about him a lot. Hell, I even think I might be falling in love with him. But it's hard to let go of the past, you know? So he's being patient with me. His exciting news is that he no longer flies the friendly skies. He's a gate agent, just like Glen was. No more four-day trips. It's great, because we are getting to know each other. I don't know what I did to deserve him. Like I said, I'm pretty lucky. I'm just going to kick back and relax for a bit. I've got a good stash in the bank, and I don't need to work for a while. Next time I do, I'm going to be a little more careful.

After all, I don't do murders.